"So you're really going to marry the man who catches you running down that mountain?"

Skye was silent for a moment, thinking. "I suppose I'd have to," she said. "But it's not likely to happen. No one's caught me yet. And I don't know how long I'll go on playing the game."

Suddenly Cole's voice took on a low, dangerous quality. "What would happen if someone from outside the settlement caught you?"

"I . . . I don't know. I never thought about it."

"I'll bet I could catch you."

She laughed out loud. "You couldn't."

"I could."

Dear Reader,

Welcome to Silhouette—experience the magic of the wonderful world where two people fall in love. Meet heroines who will make you cheer for their happiness, and heroes (be they the boy next door or a handsome, mysterious stranger) who will win your heart. Silhouette Romance reflects the magic of love—sweeping you away with books that will make you laugh and cry, heartwarming, poignant stories that will move you time and time again.

In the coming months we're publishing romances by many of your all-time favorites, such as Diana Palmer, Brittany Young, Sondra Stanford and Annette Broadrick. Your response to these authors and our other Silhouette Romance authors has served as a touchstone for us, and we're pleased to bring you more books with Silhouette's distinctive medley of charm, wit and—above all—*romance*.

I hope you enjoy this book and the many stories to come. Experience the magic!

Sincerely,

Tara Hughes
Senior Editor
Silhouette Books

ERIKA FAVOR

Mountain Home

Published by Silhouette Books New York

America's Publisher of Contemporary Romance

For my mother

SILHOUETTE BOOKS
300 E. 42nd St., New York, N.Y. 10017

ISBN: 0-373-08678-4

First Silhouette Books printing October 1989

Printed in the U.S.A.

ERIKA FAVOR

loves romance and adventure in all forms—including movies, novels and her own life. She grew up in Ohio, but now lives with two pet birds in Boulder, Colorado. When she's not writing, she's usually outdoors camping, hiking or fishing. Sometimes wanderlust leads her farther afield: recently she traveled to Spain and Portugal! In quieter moods, she likes reading, cooking for friends and spending evenings by the fire.

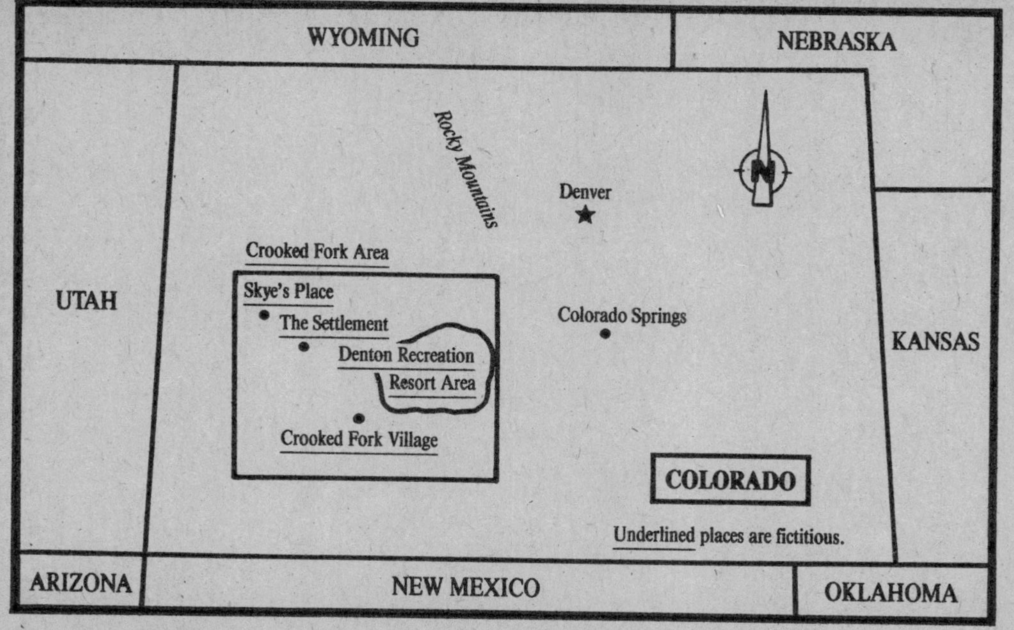
WYOMING
NEBRASKA
Rocky Mountains
Denver
Crooked Fork Area
Skye's Place
The Settlement
Denton Recreation
Resort Area
Crooked Fork Village
UTAH
Colorado Springs
KANSAS
COLORADO
Underlined places are fictitious.
ARIZONA
NEW MEXICO
OKLAHOMA

Chapter One

"There! There she goes!"

"Where?"

The young man pushed his glasses up by the nosepiece and pointed toward a row of pines on the distant mountainside. "She's running along the creek," he said.

Lifting his high-powered binoculars, Cole Denton scanned the rugged landscape in front of him. A sudden movement in his field of vision revealed the runner to him.

As he focused the lenses on the fleet-footed creature, he drew in his breath sharply. Lord, she was gorgeous! He could see her feminine curves clearly under the snug cotton dress she wore, and her long, coal-black hair streamed out behind her in a cloud of silk. But it was the expression on her face that caught and held his attention. She wore a look of pure, spontaneous joy as she leaped from stone to stone, picking her way skillfully through the thick underbrush of the mountainside.

With an effort Cole brought himself back to the situation at hand. "She's the one who's been causing you all the problems?" he asked the young man skeptically. "She's not much more than a child!"

The younger man cleared his throat, and when he spoke his voice was defensive. "She may look like a child, but she's got some sort of power among the locals here. They do what she says. I'm not positive, but I suspect she's the ringleader of the group that's been disrupting our work."

"I can see why the men would pay her a lot of attention, at any rate," Cole said, his binoculars trained again on the girl running down the mountainside. "Hey, there's some guy following her."

"That's the game, I guess," explained the younger man. "She starts out from her cabin way up on the mountainside every Monday morning. When she passes that bunch of cabins halfway down the mountain—they call it the settlement—one or two of the men who live there takes off after her. Or so they told me." He peered through his own binoculars at the distant pair. "Yeah, that's Tom Zale. He follows her a lot."

"I don't get it." Cole was annoyed with the whole situation. "You mean grown men chase this girl down the mountain—as a game?"

"It's some sort of tradition." Sighing, the younger man lowered his binoculars. "I've tried to get them to stop—they run straight through Denton Recreation's property, and they never pay attention to the trails. I'm worried about possible lawsuits if one of them gets hurt. These mountains are full of rattlesnakes."

Cole nodded, still watching the girl. She wore only leather sandals on her feet, and while they looked sturdy, y still weren't the sort of protection necessary in snake ıntry.

'They never catch her, either."

'What? Oh, the men who chase her." He looked at the e with new interest. The man following the young man seemed to move quickly, and for a moment he ned on her. But she shot across the creek and into a :ket of bushes, and within minutes he was far behind . Cole could clearly see the expression of frustration the man's face as he recognized the futility of the se.

nexplicably, Cole was glad she hadn't been caught. en he wrenched his mind back into its usual business de and turned to the young man beside him.

'Okay, Joe," he said. "Thanks for filling me in. You head back to Denver to find out your next assign-nt."

'I'm real sorry, Mr. Denton," Joe said, pushing up his sses again. "I hope I won't be demoted at Denton creation because of the way things turned out here."

'We'll see," Cole said noncommittally. Joe had good entions, but it had been a mistake to put a straight-out-college newcomer in charge of an operation. He made iental note to tell his brother that Joe needed a pro-assignment that already had a clear leader estab-ied.

As the younger man walked dejectedly out of the small in, Cole remembered an earlier question. "What did say her name was?"

'Skye. Skye Archer."

After Joe left, Cole stared moodily at the mountain-e where the pair of runners had disappeared from nt. He didn't want this job. Didn't want to cope with problems caused by an inexperienced man's mistakes and the childish tricks that some locals were playing. But his sense of fairness had told him that his younger brother was right when he'd insisted Cole come out and solve this problem personally.

"You've been driving the workers nuts, Cole," John had told him bluntly. "You're pushing everyone way too hard, including yourself. I know you're still angry about Deidre, but—"

"That's got nothing to do with it," Cole had interrupted. But now, looking back, he recognized that the way Deidre had tossed him aside *had* hurt his pride, even though he'd never been in love with her. While he'd understood her youthful desire to stretch her wings, she hadn't had to do it with his own employees.

"Besides," he'd continued, ignoring the skeptical look on his brother's face, "I don't want to spend time in the backwoods to solve problems that any competent employee could have handled easily."

"The problem's more serious than we realized," John had told him. "The people in the area are actually sabotaging the new facility we're working on, and the tourists are being frightened away by all the hostility." He'd paused, a faraway look in his eyes. "You know, Cole, Crooked Fork, Colorado is just the kind of thing we want to specialize in: resort area construction. And this could be big enough to get Denton Rec way ahead and out of the danger zone for good. But if we don't get things cleared up with the locals, it will never swing."

"Why don't you go and take care of it, then? You know I'm happier in the city." It wasn't the city so much as the fast pace of life there that appealed to him; he'd been called a workaholic, but work wasn't a negative addiction for him—he thrived on it.

'Because I need to be here with the architects to work the Springs resort plans," John had said. "You're the : who's good in the field. Besides, it'll do you and your od pressure a heap of good to get out and breathe ne mountain air. It might even make you human ain."

Cole had reluctantly agreed to take on the job, but now wished he hadn't. It was so damned quiet here! He ked around the rustic cabin that was to be his home the upcoming summer months and sighed heavily. e place was made for relaxation, but he didn't feel like ting his feet up.

He headed out the door. There was no time like the sent to check out the local people's real attitudes to- rd the new recreational facility in their village. And to d out if this Skye Archer was, in fact, a ringleader of saboteurs.

As Skye reached the bottom of the mountain, she wed her pace to a sedate walk. Now inside the edges of village, the unofficial race was over.

She reached inside her large denim bag to check on her tches. They were safe, undamaged by the breathless down the mountain. She smiled to herself in relief. ey were the best she'd done yet, and she was sure that souvenir shop would be able to sell them for her.

As she walked, she looked around at the sleepy moun- n village. It was still early, and few of the small shops d opened their doors yet. She grimaced as she saw the ge orange crane off to her right. "Denton Recrea- n," she muttered aloud. She turned away from the in- sive sight.

Suddenly she felt a strong hand grip her shoulder. Instinctively she recoiled from the unfamiliar touch and spun around.

Her gaze traveled up from the broad chest before her and locked with the coldest set of gray eyes she'd ever seen. She shuddered involuntarily. "What do you want?"

"To talk to you. Come on, I'll buy you a cup of coffee."

The owner of the cold gray eyes was a stranger, yet he didn't look like one of the tourists who'd been coming around the village with increasing frequency these days. He looked strong, with broad shoulders and large hands, and his dark hair had only the faintest trace of gray at the temples. His sport coat and lightweight wool pants looked more elegant and sophisticated than most of the residents of Crooked Fork—or most of the tourists, for that matter—could afford. But for all his high-class appearance, he was a stranger, and Skye didn't like his tone.

"I don't know you," she said. "And I don't need any strange men to buy me coffee."

"We've got some business to discuss," he said. His eyes left hers and skimmed over her body, then met hers again. Although the masculine once-over was subtle, Skye recognized it for what it was and felt flustered.

"I don't know of any business with you."

"Come on inside and I'll explain." He took her arm to steer her toward the coffee shop.

The confident tone of his voice irked her, as did the slightly condescending touch on her arm. He wasn't even going to tell her what he wanted; he just assumed she'd go with him.

But Skye Archer hadn't taken orders from anyone for more than two years—since her grandmother had died—

l she didn't intend to start now. Her immediate prob- a was to get rid of the hand gripping her arm.

She moved along with him toward the coffee shop, ,ging her moment. When he felt her moving beside a, he relaxed his hold on her.

n a flash she twisted away from him and ran up the ps that led to Bob's souvenir shop. From the shop's ·ch, safely behind the railing, she looked down at the man's surprised face. She couldn't resist a grin of ımph at her easy escape.

'Hey, come on back here,'' he said. ''I wasn't going ıurt you. I just want to talk to you.''

Her grin deepened as she noticed that all the arro- ıce was gone from his voice. ''I don't go places with ıngers,'' she called down to him. ''I have too much to '' Her heart pounding, she slipped through the door the souvenir shop.

She was still wondering at her own reaction to him as : worked later that afternoon in her cabin. The sun nted through the wide-open windows, and the air that fted in was fresh and fragrant with pine.

nhaling appreciatively, Skye leaned back from her tch pad. She'd had the cabin closed up for much of winter, and the fresh air was a welcome change that naled spring's arrival, at last.

Her thoughts drifted back to her encounter with the y-eyed stranger this morning, and she shook her head. s subtle and very masculine scrutiny of her kept flash- before her, making her feel strangely uncomfortable. ıat had he wanted with her? And why had she felt so settled with him—she, the one who was always calm l serene? When her friends had gone dreamy-eyed over nage boys, she'd never felt a flicker of puppy love.

When problems or emergencies caused other people to fly off the handle, she could be counted on to keep her head and do the right thing. So why had this complete stranger made her feel so shaken?

Forget about it, she told herself firmly, and turned back to the charcoal drawing before her. The image of a young deer, inspired by a fawn she'd found last year and raised herself, was coming to life.

A knock on the door made her pause.

"Come in," she called. Farimer hadn't barked, so the caller had to be someone she knew.

The door opened. "Hi, Skye, it's me."

"Lynnie!" In an instant Skye was on her feet and across the rough-hewn floor to greet her oldest friend. "You're back!"

She embraced the blond-haired woman, then stepped back to look at her. Immediately she noticed Lyn's swelling pregnancy, and met her eyes. "How long?" she asked.

"Early June," Lyn said, and then sank down onto one of the oak chairs by the dining room table. "That's why we came back. Bob couldn't find a job in Denver, and with this being our third. . . ."

Skye nodded sympathetically. Here on the mountain, Lyn and Bob would at least be among family who could help them out, despite the fact that there was little hope for Bob to find steady work here.

She listened as her friend described their six-month stay in Denver, which had ended in failure. Poor Lyn! She was only twenty-two, and yet she had two small children, another on the way, and an unemployed husband. The hard times showed, too; Lyn's face was lined and there were dark circles under her eyes that bespoke sleepless nights.

"But you haven't heard the latest gossip at the settle-ent," Lyn was saying, and Skye leaned forward, grin-ıg, as she caught the twinkle in the blond woman's es. Skye had little company up here at the cabin, and n's quick tongue was welcome to her.

"Guess what Tom Zale's saying about you."

"Oh, no, what?"

"He's thinking about giving up the chase. He wants to k you to marry him, anyway."

"You're kidding!" Skye heard the squeal in her own ice. "Who told you that?"

The blond woman shifted into a more comfortable sition. "The settlement's buzzing about it, Skye. ıey're so nosy where you're concerned. Some of the l-timers don't think it's right."

Skye brushed her hair back, feeling impatient. "The ase is getting ridiculous. Just because Mama and andma found husbands that way doesn't mean I have Times are changing."

"But I thought you believed in the chase," Lyn said. 'om said you told him that you'd marry him if he could tch you."

"I did tell him that, a long time ago. But only because new he couldn't catch me running down that moun-n. None of the men could."

Lyn surveyed her friend, an expression of certainty in r eyes. "Someday there'll come a man who can keep up th you. And when he does, you'll know it."

As Lyn went on filling in other settlement gossip she'd ard, Skye's mind wandered. She didn't really want to arry Tom. But the prospects in the settlement were de-ledly limited, and she wanted a family eventually. Even ough Lyn had a hard time with her two children, Skye vied her sometimes.

"Who's got your babies this afternoon?" she asked when Lyn paused for breath.

"Mother's home, so she's watching them. That's how I heard all this about Tom." She paused and looked down at her rounded belly. "I wish you'd deliver this one, too, Skye, like you did Sarah and Jason." She looked at her friend pleadingly. "I'd feel so much better knowing you'd take care of things for me."

"I just don't feel right about it anymore. Not by myself."

"But you know exactly what to do."

"In most cases, sure. I was with Gran on almost every delivery she made. But now we've got the hospital just twenty miles away, and it's safer. If something goes wrong, they've got the right equipment to handle it."

"But I don't want to go back into a city. I hate the noise and rush."

Skye almost laughed. The city where the new hospital was located hardly deserved the name; she'd learned that during her two-year stint at college in Denver. But people like Lyn never got used to city life, and in fact, that was probably the real reason she and Bob hadn't made it in the city and had had to come home.

She leaned toward her friend. "You're just going to have to put up with it," she said firmly. "I want you to have your baby in the hospital where it's safest. Now, tell me how you've been feeling."

"Terrible, in the mornings," Lyn admitted. "It's the nausea again. But afternoons and evenings, I feel pretty good."

"I'll give you some tea that will help," she said, turning toward the cupboard quickly to hide her frown. It was late in the pregnancy for Lyn to be feeling nauseous, and she was glad she'd insisted that Lyn have the baby in town. She had a bad feeling about Lyn's overall health.

She busied herself measuring out herbs from two containers. "Here," she said, handing the small package to Lyn. "Brew a spoonful of this in two cups of water and drink it every morning. And be sure to have two pieces of toast or some cereal with it."

"Okay, Doc."

Skye hoped she'd follow the instructions. The mild peppermint and fennel would help with the nausea, but even more important was the breakfast. She knew that Lyn tended to skip meals, especially when she was tense or worried. But her friend also believed strongly in Skye's herbal medicines, and that very belief might help her combat the nausea.

A car door slammed, and then Farimer's staccato barking burst through the quiet cabin's open windows, startling both women. Strangers were rare this high up the mountain, but that was the only thing likely to make the dog bark so hysterically.

Skye hurried to the door and peered out, but the path to her doorway was overgrown, and she couldn't see anyone.

"Call off your dog, will you?"

The rough, annoyed voice made Skye's heart pound. It was the man from this morning.

Lyn had been peering over her shoulder, so together they emerged from the cabin and started down the path toward the sound of Farimer's growling. When they saw what the dog was doing, they both stopped abruptly; then, looking at each other, they giggled.

Farimer was crouched low, snarling, his hair bristling at the back of his neck. The tall man held a thick stick that Farimer had gripped at the other end, and the two were having a tug of war with it, Farimer growling all the time.

When he heard the two women laughing, the stranger dropped his end of the stick. Farimer looked back once at his mistress, then loped off into the woods with the stick.

"That beast didn't look so funny from close quarters," he said, his voice laced with irritation. "Is he yours?"

Skye nodded, still unable to restrain a grin. "Sorry to laugh. It's just that sticks are his favorite toy, and he thought you were playing with him."

The stranger frowned and brushed the dirt off his hands onto the sides of his pants. "I need to talk to you. Seriously."

She hesitated only a minute. His presence evoked a tiny sense of unease she could feel in the pit of her stomach. But, after all, the man had driven all the way up the mountain on a rutted dirt road and had been subjected to Farimer's fierce-seeming attack; the least she could do was invite him in and listen to what he had to say. "Come on in," she said, turning back toward the cabin.

"I guess I should head on down, Skye," Lyn said, and they all paused. "But first, could you..." She trailed off the sentence, looking at the stranger.

"What do you need?" Skye asked her.

"Do you think you could . . . say words over the baby? Like you did for Jason and Sarah?"

Skye stole a glimpse at the stranger. He said nothing, but she saw the curiosity blaze in his eyes. When she met her friend's pleading expression, she made her decision immediately.

"Of course." She turned back to the stranger. "Just go on inside and have a seat. I'll be right in."

She put an arm around Lyn's shoulder and walked a few more paces down the path. Under one of the tall pines, she paused. "Stand here," she said. She knelt down before Lyn's swelling belly and placed her hands on it. Closing her eyes, she concentrated on the new life there and whispered a short prayer for the child's health. As she finished, she felt the baby kick in the womb.

"He moved! I know everything's going to be okay now," Lyn said softly. "Thanks, Skye."

The two friends embraced, then Lyn started down the trail. "Be careful now," Skye called after her, then turned back toward the cabin.

The man stood on the porch, watching her every move.

Skye flushed as she walked toward him. He'd seen her speak over the baby. And she was certain that he hadn't understood what he'd seen—few people would, unless they'd grown up with similar traditions. The customs on the mountain went far back, some coming from the pioneer families that had settled here over a century ago, and some from the Indians who had traveled this countryside for hundreds of years.

And she, as part of a line of midwives and herb doctors descended from those first settlers, was smack in the middle of most of the country traditions. She sometimes had her doubts about them; she didn't know whether her "words" would help Lyn's baby grow strong and healthy or not. But she did know that Lyn's frame of mind was as important as any medicine, and Lyn believed strongly in her friend's "magic" hands.

She started up the wooden steps to her front door, then paused and looked up at the unmoving man in front of her. She'd thought his eyes looked cold before, but now there was something in them that suggested fire, not ice.

She felt her heart pound as she stepped past him and opened the cabin door.

"Are you the resident priest?" he asked. "Or witch doctor?"

The words stung. Although she had her own questions about some of the mountain traditions, questions that came from a lifetime of wide reading and two years of college life, she didn't like outsiders making fun of the customs. Deep inside she sensed the value of the herbal remedies and of the sort of blessings her grandmother had taught her to say over unborn children. Her back stiff, she looked up at the stranger.

"I asked you to go inside. I meant for you not to watch."

"You're . . . interesting to watch."

Skye bit her lip in annoyance. He made her sound like some exotic amoeba he'd just isolated under the microscope. "Go on in and have a seat," she said, hearing the tightness in her own voice. She followed him in. "What did you want to talk with me about?"

"Why did you run away from me this morning?"

"I didn't run away."

His eyebrows shot up in exaggerated surprise. "You didn't? What would you call it, then?"

She shrugged. No point in getting in a useless argument over words. Let him carry the conversation. He was the stranger; he was the one who'd have to explain himself.

He eyed her narrowly for a moment. Then he switched subjects abruptly. "Do you know who I am?"

She shook her head.

"I'm Cole Denton."

She stiffened. "As in Denton Recreation?"

He nodded. "That's right. I'm here because the previous manager couldn't keep things under control. We need to get the cooperation of the villagers if Denton is ever going to be able to build up a good business here. That means the sabotage has to end."

"Sabotage?"

"Yes. Don't act naive. Joe told me you were involved in tampering with Denton equipment. According to him, you were something of a ringleader."

The nerve of such a statement! Skye bit back a sharp answer and stared out the window into the trees. Suddenly she could hear her grandmother's voice as if the woman were in the room. "Nature cures all man-made ills," she used to say when Skye was having trouble with her friends.

Skye watched the gentle, waving movements of the treetops in the wind. Then she turned back to the impatient man before her. "I don't know if you're going to believe me or not. But I didn't have anything to do with damaging your equipment. I didn't even know about it, beyond a few rumors."

"Didn't you, now?"

"No." His sarcasm made her want to hurt him. "But I will tell you one thing, Mr. Denton," she continued. "No one on this mountain likes what Denton Recreation is doing to our land and our lives. We've been here for generations, most of us, and we don't like all the changes that have happened since Denton Rec brought its ugly equipment in to start building this big resort."

Cole sighed and shook his head as if he'd heard this argument before. "Nobody ever wants change, Skye. But the world is changing. This place was bound to be discovered sometime. And Denton will at least make the attempt to keep the land in a natural state. If a mining company had come in, the same might not be true."

"That's just an excuse. Someone else would have done it anyway, so it might as well be you who makes a fortune out of destroying innocent people's land."

"Dammit, that's not how it is at all." Cole was on his feet and standing too close to her, and before she could help herself she stepped backward. There was some kind of raw power in him that made her uncomfortable, and that feeling wasn't familiar to Skye.

To hide her discomfort she turned away and started straightening her art supplies, willing herself to stay calm. But the movements of her hands were jerky and she hoped he wouldn't notice.

"You live here alone?"

She hesitated, suddenly wishing she could deny it. If only Gran were still alive and would be coming through the door any minute, she wouldn't have this nervous feeling inside. But wishing wouldn't make it so. "Yes, I've lived alone for almost two years," she said finally.

"Aren't you afraid?"

"Of what?"

"Of...I don't know, crime and men getting out of hand. Where I come from, young girls don't usually live alone."

She laughed. "I'm not a young girl, I'm twenty-two. And we don't have much crime around here."

"Twenty-two, are you? I'd never have guessed it. You look sixteen." He studied her face, then his eyes swept down over her in that subtle once-over she'd noticed this morning. "Well, maybe not sixteen. But young."

She blushed, and then a wave of anger washed over her. Who was this man to come into her home and make her feel uncomfortable? Even though he was subtle about it—more subtle than some of the Denton construction workers had been when she'd walked by—he was still looking her over as if she were nothing more than a sex object. And his description of her as "young" was patronizing.

"Age doesn't always bring wisdom, Mr. Denton."

"You can call me Cole. I'm not that ancient myself."

She glanced up at him, noticing again the trace of gray in his hair. But he wasn't really old looking despite the gray; there was too much restless energy in the way he held himself and the tight muscles visible under his shirt. Some of the men on the mountain looked stooped and old before their time, beaten down by a life of hard work that still barely fed their families. It was obvious that this man hadn't had that sort of experience.

"Maybe I'm more ancient than I realized," he said, and she looked at his face, startled out of her thoughts. There was a curious look in his eyes, one that was hard to read. She thought he looked a little sad.

"Of course you're not old... Cole. But you've got a few things to learn about Crooked Fork."

He'd smiled when she'd called him by his first name, but the smile disappeared when he heard the rest of her statement. "Such as?"

"We like our life here, and we don't want someone trying to change it. If you stay and keep trying, you're going to keep having problems."

"Is that a threat?" His powerful shoulders flexed slightly, stretching his shirt at the seams.

She shrugged her shoulders. "Not from me. Whatever you think, I haven't done anything physical to Denton's equipment. But I can't speak for all my neighbors, and everyone's unhappy with the way things are going."

"You people are all the same. Never wanting your lives to change, and then wondering why you're dirt poor and out of touch with the twentieth century."

"All the same! We're all the same! That just shows—" she walked to the door and opened it "—you're more ignorant and prejudiced than the least educated child at the settlement. And I don't think I've got anything more to discuss with you."

He drew in his breath sharply at the way she was ushering him out, but she noticed that he wasn't being patronizing anymore. "Listen here, lady," he said. "You tell your people that sabotage is a crime, and we're not going to put up with it any longer."

"I'll mention it."

"You'd better take me seriously, and you'd better do more than mention it."

She didn't respond, and after a frustrated glare he plunged out of the cabin and down the path.

Chapter Two

kye! Come quick!"

At the sound of the small child's panicked voice, Skye rned from the counter at the Sunshine General Store. What is it, Sam?"

"Me an' Ricky were playing over at the site an' Ricky ll down, an' there's blood all over—" His voice choked with tears, and he rubbed a small dirty fist across his ce.

"Show me where." She dropped her packages on the unter and ran after the child. In minutes they were at e site of Denton Recreation's latest building project. am led the way through some tangled bushes at the far de of the site, where the protective fence was broken own.

There, on a pile of glass and steel shavings, lay little icky Zale, Tom Zale's nephew. He was still and pale, d a gaping wound in his leg streamed blood.

Sam began to wail afresh at the sight of his helpless friend. Skye knelt down in front of him, gripped him firmly by the shoulders, and shook him gently. "Sam, listen to me. You're going to have to do something very grown up."

The child's eyes widened and his wailing stopped.

"I want you to run over to where those men are." She pointed at a distant group of men in orange hard hats. "Tell them to bring a truck over here right away to help Ricky. You'll have to ride with them to show them where we are."

"But . . . but I don't know them . . ."

Skye sighed in exasperation. The tiny village they called the settlement was so small and ingrown that its children were often shy of strangers. "I know you don't know them, but you want to help Ricky, don't you? You have to be brave."

Sam gulped, then nodded.

"Go on. And be careful." She gave him a light push and he ran toward the group of men.

Immediately she turned her attention to young Ricky, who still hadn't moved. The wound on his leg was the most immediate problem, and she fumbled hastily through her denim bag for something she could use to staunch the bleeding. But there was nothing suitable. Without hesitation she ripped two long strips of fabric from the bottom of her skirt. One of them she wadded up and pressed hard against the wound, making sure the edges of skin were close together. The other she used to tie the first in place. Applying firm pressure to the wound, she used her other hand to feel the child's limbs.

Nothing seemed to be broken, and she decided that he'd probably passed out from the pain and the sight of blood. Moving carefully, she eased him off the pile of ıvings and glass and lay him on the neighboring grass. ɛ slipped off her overshirt and put it over him to keep n warm.

At the sound of a pickup's roaring motor behind her, ye stood in relief. The stubble-faced man driving it nped out and looked at her appreciatively. "What can o for you, pretty lady?" His eyes widened as he stared · up and down, and Skye realized that her medical at- tion to Ricky had left her considerably less clothed ın she had been when she'd come into town that ›rning. She wore only her snug T-shirt and newly ›rtened skirt she'd made the bandages from. But her f-consciousness wasn't the most important issue now; ;ky was,

"This child is badly hurt. We need to get him to the spital." Her voice, crisp and businesslike, seemed to t the man out of his admiration of her too revealing thes. He looked down at the pale child and then met · eyes again, and there was the faintest hint of apol- y in his voice.

"Sure, I'll help. What should I do?"

"We need to lift him into the truck as carefully as we ı. I don't want to move him any more than necessary case something's broken."

They each slid their hands under the child, the stub- -faced man taking Ricky's shoulders while she sup- rted his wounded leg. Moving slowly, they slid the ld onto the pickup's front seat.

Sam ran beside them. "Can I go to the hospital, too?"

Skye turned to him as soon as Ricky was safely in the ck. "No, Sam, you can't. I need you to do another portant job."

The child's chest swelled. "Sure. What do you want me do?"

"Do you know where Ricky's mom is?"

The child frowned, trying to remember. "I think she's visiting with my mom up home."

She knelt down in front of him and gripped his shoulders. "Okay, honey. I want you to run back up to the settlement as fast as you can. Tell Ricky's mom what happened, and tell her he's going to be all right." She emphasized the last words, and Sam nodded vigorously. "Tell her we took him to the hospital at High Mesa." She made him repeat the hospital name, then watched as he ran off at full speed, puffed up with his important errand.

"Don't you folks have phones up there?" the stubble-faced man asked. His eyes strayed down the length of her again.

"No, it costs too much to get the lines this far," she explained, flushing a little under his scrutiny. "Most of the people can't afford it. Now, could we—"

"What's going on?"

She turned toward the voice. Cole Denton stood there, hands on hips, dressed in a hard hat and work clothes, and she saw his eyes rake quickly over her before he turned to look inquiringly at the stubble-faced worker.

"I dunno, Mr. Denton. Something happened—"

"Ricky Zale hurt himself on your nice little pile of glass and steel shavings," she interrupted, gesturing toward the still-unconscious boy on the truck's front seat. "We're taking him to the hospital at High Mesa."

In an instant he'd taken in the whole situation, his eyes moving from the injured child to the pile of shavings to the stubble-faced man's slight leer. "I'll drive you there," he said immediately. "Stretch, you can get back to work. Thanks for the help."

"But I—"

'I'll take care of it."

'he man nodded with resignation and started walking k toward the other workers.

'Get in and hold the child steady," Cole said abruptly ıe walked around to the driver's side and got in. An- at his tone, but recognizing his concern for Ricky, 'e climbed awkwardly into the passenger's side and ·lt on the floor, her arms curved protectively over the r's still form.

'he drive to the hospital was quiet except for Skye's ;e directions. High Mesa was twenty miles away on stly mountain roads, but Cole's fast, competent driv- got them there quickly. As they screeched up to the ergency room's entrance, Ricky began to moan qui- . Skye relaxed her pressure on the leg wound and ıded him over to two white-clad nurses inside the hos- ıl.

'Looks like you did a pretty good job taking care of t kid," said Cole as they sank into adjoining chairs in waiting room.

'He should never have been hurt. That construction is completely unsafe."

Cole frowned. "How did they get in, anyway?"

'The fence is broken. The kids may have torn it down mselves," she admitted, "but even so, it's Denton :'s responsibility to make sure that the fence stays re- red. You know how kids are. They're fascinated with kind of workplace, and they're bound to try and get ,

Ie nodded. "You're right that we should have kept the ce in better repair. And if I'd been in charge all along, would have."

"You're really concerned with the townspeople and their well-being, aren't you?" Her voice was deliberately sarcastic.

"Dammit, yes, I am!" His hands clenched into fists. "Denton Rec is known for taking good care of the residents in any place we develop. We always try to hire locals, and we keep the environmental impact as light as is humanly possible. That's why things like this infuriate me. It's sheer incompetence on the part of that clown who was trying to run things before."

Skye shrugged and let the matter drop. He did sound sincere, but she didn't trust him.

A few minutes passed in silence. Skye went to the desk to see if there was any news on Ricky, and the nurse in charge went back toward the treatment rooms to check on him.

As Skye walked back toward Cole, he was looking at her clothes in a way that made her flush, and when she sat down beside him she picked up a magazine and pretended he wasn't there. Or tried to.

He cleared his throat. "Ah, that outfit."

She flipped over two more pages in the magazine before she looked up at him, waiting for him to go on. She'd managed, in that short space of time, to control her embarrassment to some extent.

"It's, well, different from the other clothes I've seen you wear." To her surprise, he looked embarrassed himself.

"What do you mean?"

"It's . . . it's more . . ."

"More what?"

"More sexy, dammit!" He'd heard the amusement in her voice. "It's pretty revealing, and I'm not complaining. But you ought to be careful about wearing that kind hing around the site. Some of the men who work for can be a little rough, and when you come around se kind of men dressed like that, you're just inviting ıble for yourself."

he put the magazine down hard on the table beside . "I wasn't dressed like this when I went out this rning. I had to use my overshirt to cover Ricky, and bottom of this skirt was the only thing I had to bind his cut. Believe me, I wouldn't go around your work- trying to get their attention. The way those men gawk kes me sick."

'They're only human, Skye. Sometimes the work they gets monotonous. And then a woman as pretty as you ks by, and it's the most exciting thing that's hap- ıed to them all day."

he picked the magazine back up, pretending indiffer- e to what he'd said. So he thought she was pretty. She n't like the man's sometimes patronizing attitude, and hated what he stood for. So why did the thought that iked the way she looked give her a sense of warmth in pit of her stomach?

'he nurse came toward them. "Ricky's going to be ," she said. "But they had to give him some stitches, he's under sedation. He'll need to stay here for a ple of hours. Then you can take him home."

kye nodded, not bothering to explain that Ricky n't her child, and the nurse went away.

'What's going on, Skye? Where's my Ricky?"

'he high, frightened voice cut through the quiet wait- room as Ricky's mother ran toward them. Tom Zale owed almost as quickly.

'It's okay. He's going to be fine," Skye said, stand- up to put her arm around the woman. Quickly she nmed up what had happened and what the nurse had just said. But the anxious mother wouldn't rest until she'd seen her son, so Skye took her to the nurse, who led her back down the hallway toward the treatment rooms.

When she walked back she saw Tom Zale's eyes on her, and the open admiration in them made her flush. Darn this outfit. Glancing at Cole, she saw that he'd noticed the other man's reaction.

"You brought Wanda down?" she asked Tom, trying to ignore the way his eyes kept straying down to her too small T-shirt.

He nodded. "I was at the house when Sam came up hollering about what had happened to Ricky. Wanda was all broken up, so I drove her here. But how'd you and Ricky get here?"

With an odd nervousness she turned toward Cole and introduced the two men. Immediately a veiled animosity flared between them. Tom had always considered himself to be Skye's protector, ever since they were kids together, and for the past year he'd been hinting that his feelings ran deeper. Now he seemed to sense a rival in the older man.

"I can run you home, Skye," Tom said, turning to her. "You don't want to wait here all afternoon, do you?"

"I'll take her home," said Cole smoothly. "You'll need to wait for Ricky and his mother, of course."

Tom glared at the older man, then turned to Skye. "Can I talk to you for a minute?"

"Sure," she said, suppressing a sigh, and he took her arm and led her a short distance down the hospital corridor. They were out of Cole's earshot but not out of his sight, and she could sense him watching them out of the corner of his eye.

"You'd better look out for that guy," Tom said. "He's up to something where you're concerned."

Her lips tightened. "That's nonsense. He's just worried because an accident happened on his site, to a little kid. Anyone would have done what he did."

Tom shook his head. "You don't know much about the world, sweetheart. I can tell from the way he looks at you that he's got trouble on his mind."

"I'm not a child! I can take care of myself."

"Sure you can, sure you can." His soothing tone only irritated her more. "But, honey," he continued, "I don't want you to have to take care of yourself. I've been wanting to talk to you about that."

When he put his hands on her shoulders and moved closer she backed away, uncomfortable. She didn't want to hear Tom plead with her, and she didn't want Cole to watch the whole exchange.

"This isn't the time or the place," she said.

He looked at her a minute, then nodded. "All right. We won't talk about it now. But let's get together next week, okay?"

She hesitated. In the past she'd tried to keep her dates with Tom minimal because she didn't want him to get too many serious ideas about her. But they'd known each other for such a long time that she didn't want to insult him by turning cold.

She'd learned from her grandmother that there were many kinds of love one could have for a person. Despite the fact that she didn't love Tom romantically, she valued their long friendship. And though she'd never had a brother, she imagined that what she felt for Tom was what a sister might feel.

"Sure, Tom," she said. "That will be nice. Why don't you come over for dinner Saturday night?"

"Great." He pulled her against him and gave her a quick, hard kiss. Then he strode down the hall past the waiting area and headed for the room where Ricky and his sister, Wanda, were.

Skye rolled her eyes. Men! She and Tom had kissed a few times before, and she'd never found the sensation unpleasant—though she'd never felt moved to go any further, either. But never before had Tom kissed her in public, and she knew he'd done it as a way of making a claim on her in front of Cole.

And if he'd wanted to get Cole's goat, she realized as she walked back toward the waiting room, he'd definitely succeeded. Cole's eyes were blazing as he looked up at her. "A little lover's quarrel?"

"Never mind," she said. "Let's go."

He stood up and handed her the shirt she'd used to cover Ricky earlier. "The nurse brought this out. You might want to put it on." He looked in the direction Tom had gone, then back at her. "That outfit you're wearing seems to be giving everyone ideas."

She donned the shirt hastily, glaring at him.

The ride back was silent, with both of them lost in thought. Skye wasn't at all sure of what to think of this man. He was her enemy in a sense because he stood for Denton Recreation; he was responsible for all the dirty machinery and the strangers that were invading her peaceful community. And he treated her as though she were responsible for the problems he was having. Yet his gray eyes and lean, hard body excited her, and she found herself stealing more than one glance at him as they drove.

"Where do you want to go?" he asked as they pulled into the village.

"Sunshine General Store. I left some packages there when I went to help Ricky this morning."

"And they'll still be there?"

"Of course," she replied, puzzled. "Why shouldn't they be?"

He laughed. "No reason, I guess. You don't have theft here in Crooked Fork, do you?"

"Not much," she said as they pulled up into the store's gravel parking lot. Cole got out with her, explaining that he had to buy supplies for the next few days.

"Skye, little lady. How are you?"

She blinked in the store's dim light, craning her neck to see the owner of the shaky voice. "Hi, Pops Jones," she said when she had located the old man. "How's your rheumatism today?"

"Not so good, not so good at all. I'm thinking we'll have a bad storm tonight. The air is damp."

"Have you been using that liniment I gave you?"

Pops poked at a piece of dirt with his cane. "No, I haven't," he said. "I ran out a couple of weeks ago."

"Why didn't you tell me right away?" she asked in a scolding voice. "I'll bring you some down tomorrow."

"Now, don't be doing that, little lady. You know I can't pay you for it these days." He turned and shuffled back into the storeroom before she had a chance to reply.

Skye shook her head, exasperated. She could get by well enough on her sketches and the small savings account Gran had left her; there was no need for someone like Pops, who'd been her friend for years, to go around in pain because he was too proud to accept any help unless he could pay for it. She resolved to bring him some of the liniment tomorrow.

"Ready to go?" Cole's voice at her side startled her. He must have heard the whole exchange. And he was probably laughing inwardly about her "witch doctor" status again.

She turned to him. "You don't need to wait for me. I can get home under my own steam."

"I want to drive you," he said in a firm voice and looking down at her load of supplies, she admitted to herself that she'd be grateful for the ride.

As she directed him to the rugged mountain road that led to her place, Cole looked over at her curiously. "You really are a sort of doctor for the village and settlement people, aren't you?"

"Sort of," she said, afraid he was making fun of her again.

"But you're so young. Where did you get your training?"

She looked at him, still wary. "Nowhere that city folks would respect very much," she said. "I grew up here on the mountain, with my grandparents. Gran was the community midwife and healer for years, just like her mother before her. When you live in a small settlement with the nearest city over sixty miles away, you can't be picky about medical degrees. The women in our family have always shown a talent for medicine, and people respected that."

Cole glanced over at her as he drove. "Go on," he said.

"Gran took me along on most of her errands to visit sick people. At first it was because she didn't have a baby-sitter for me, but later I started to get interested in her work. She showed me how to gather herbs and make teas and ointments and such."

"Did she teach you how to take care of a six-inch bleeding wound, like Ricky's?"

Skye nodded. "Gran knew a lot about basic first aid. For years she was the only medical person available in these parts. Now, of course, there's the hospital at High

Mesa and a clinic in the village where a doctor comes once a week. So folks have more of a choice."

"But they still come to you first."

"A lot of them do. They're not used to hospitals or doctors, especially the older ones, and they're more comfortable with someone they know." She paused, staring out the window at the twisted pines that lined the road.

"How do you feel about being a... nurse, or whatever you'd call yourself?"

"I'm not completely comfortable with it, to tell you the truth," she said. "I went to college for two years in Denver, and it made me realize how much I had to learn about modern medicine. It also made me realize that most people would never trust their health to someone with as little education as I have."

"Why'd you leave college after only two years?" he asked as he maneuvered the truck around one of the rutted road's sharp turns.

"Gran got sick," she explained. "She needed someone to take care of her, and the people around here needed someone they could call on for sickness and childbirth and such."

He pulled into the narrow dirt driveway that led to her cabin and stopped the car. "So you got sucked into the role of community doctor without much choice."

She nodded. "I try to get people to use the new hospital and the clinic when they're seriously ill. I don't want them to be completely dependent on me like they were on Gran. And since she died before she could teach me all the stuff she knew, I'm not nearly as qualified as she was."

He nodded thoughtfully, still sitting behind the wheel.

When she realized that she'd been talking to him as if he were an old friend, Skye flushed. She really didn't know him very well, but he'd seemed understanding and he'd asked all the right questions. She had few people to really talk to, and he'd been kind to listen to her problems.

"Would you like to come in for a cup of coffee before you go back down?" she asked hesitantly. If he'd been from the area, she would have extended the invitation automatically and it would have been accepted just as automatically; being hospitable was one of the first things girl children learned on the mountain. But the big man beside her was from another culture, so she felt some doubt as she offered the traditional invitation.

His eyes revealed something like surprise as he looked at her. "That would be great," he said.

He sat at her dining table while she moved around the cabin's kitchen. When she put out a plate of bread, with butter and preserves alongside, he grinned appreciatively. "That looks homemade," he said.

"It is." She put a steaming cup of coffee in front of him and sat down.

"It's delicious. A rare treat." For several moments they munched in silence. The sun slanting through the cabin windows reminded Skye that it was midafternoon and she hadn't had any lunch. That was why she was so hungry! And one look at the way Cole was wolfing down bread and butter told her he felt the same way.

Finally, as if satiated at last, he sat back. He looked at her, a long look, and there was something in his eyes that made her feel breathless. He put out his hand to cover hers where it rested on the table.

"Thank you for feeding me," he said, tightening his hand on hers.

She couldn't break his gaze. "Of course, it's nothing," she said, and the breathlessness she felt came through in her voice.

"It's not nothing. You're a kind woman." He leaned toward her slightly and his thumb moved on her hand in a light caress.

The air between them seemed laced with anticipation, and the companionable mood in which they'd eaten had changed subtly. He was still looking at her with a depth of meaning in his eyes, and she was suddenly afraid that he was going to kiss her and she was going to let him. She pulled her hand away from his and stood up quickly.

"I'd better clear this away," she said, her voice oddly high.

"Wait." He stood up and moved to her side, and his hand touched her face when she looked up at him questioningly. He leaned down toward her slightly and then paused, looking into her eyes as if he could read every thought behind them, could read the confusion and fear and excitement that were churning around inside of her.

His hand moved to lift her face toward his, and then his lips brushed hers, softly and gently. He paused and looked at her eyes again as if to judge her reaction, and then his lips came down on hers once more, a little harder. When he lifted his head she saw the fire in his eyes.

She backed away with a tiny gasp and blindly started gathering plates and cups from the table. The way he stood still, watching her, was unnerving.

A plate slipped from her fingers and shattered on the floor.

"Darn it. I'm never this clumsy."

"Let me help." He knelt down beside her, helping her to gather the broken pieces, and his nearness made her awkward again. She winced when a sliver of pottery cut her finger.

"Is it bad? Let me see." He lifted her hand to look at the tiny cut.

"It's fine... it's hardly bleeding."

Hearing the breathlessness in her voice, he looked in her eyes again, and saw the smoldering tension still there. Holding her gaze, he slowly lifted her hand to his mouth and kissed the tiny cut.

The sensation of his lips made something twist in the pit of her stomach and she drew in her breath. This man was turning her inside out, making her feel as she'd never felt before, and her body didn't seem to understand the fact that they were enemies.

Still looking at her, he took the broken shards from her other hand and put them in the wastebasket behind him. Then he deposited the rest of the dishes on the counter.

She felt rooted to the spot, kneeling on the floor where the plate pieces had been, unable to look away from the man who was making a thousand feelings, fears and warnings whirl around inside her head. It was only when he came toward her that she started to stand up.

He reached out to help her, and when she was standing he didn't let go of her hands. There was fire in his gray eyes and she knew he was going to kiss her again, and suddenly she was afraid. She pulled back, trying to loosen her hands from the grip in which he held them.

"What's wrong, Skye?" His voice was soft, and the underlying breathlessness in it matched the way she felt.

How could she put into words the combination of fear and excitement that was making her back away? She shook her head, staring down at the rough-hewn floor.

He touched her chin, trying to get her to meet his eyes again, and after a moment's resistance she looked at him.

"Please. Let me hold you." His tone was pleading, humble, and although there was desire in his eyes he didn't move an inch toward her. He was waiting for her answer.

"I... I don't know if it's..."

"Just for a minute?" His hands tightened on hers and his eyes looked soft, liquid.

She didn't plan to nod, didn't recognize the whispered "yes" that she heard in the room as her own. But when she felt him draw her into his arms she knew it was what she wanted. She felt his body, hard and muscular, pressed gently against her softness and his big hand stroked the length of her hair, burning a path down her back.

He nuzzled the top of her head until she turned her face up toward him, wanting to feel his lips again, and he took the hint and kissed her softly, first her forehead and then her lips. The light touch seemed to inflame him and he made a sound deep in his throat.

Then he was kissing her again, harder this time, and his tongue traced the inner lines of her lips until they opened slightly. Her breathing quickened as she felt him probe her delicately, finding the most sensitive places. His arms were still around her, tracing patterns on her back, and as he kissed her more deeply he pulled her closer against his body.

They fit together as if they were made for each other, and it was instinct, not reason, that made her tighten her arms around him.

When he felt her response he started to breathe harder, his mouth moving to taste the tender skin of her neck. Skye shivered at the unfamiliar feeling. His hands were splayed wide on her back now, pressing her even closer to him, and her whole body felt strained and swollen and full of tension that demanded relief.

His mouth was close to her ear and between kisses he murmured words of tenderness to her. "You're so sweet, so loving," he whispered. Then he caught the lobe of her ear in his mouth and sucked gently. She gasped.

"Yes, that's what I want to do. I want to make you go crazy."

She felt hot, feverish, as he rained kisses down the side of her neck, and she couldn't restrain her fast breathing.

He was whispering in her ear again, intimate words she'd never heard before, and suddenly she realized where they were heading. And with that realization all her reason came back and she was shocked at what she was allowing to happen.

"No, wait," she said, still breathless as she tried to push him away.

"Oh, honey, don't stop me now." He still held her close, his lips and teeth still playing with the tender skin of her neck. "I want to make you happy."

Suddenly she was afraid, because she saw that he assumed they were going to make love. And she knew her response to him had encouraged that assumption. She twisted in his arms, pushing at his broad chest, and finally, looking dazed, he let her go.

She backed away, her hands flying to brush back her hair. Her breathing felt ragged and she knew that her face was flushed.

"Skye..."

"I'm sorry, I shouldn't have let that happen. I don't know what got into me." She was looking away from him, afraid to meet his eyes.

"Don't be embarrassed." He stepped toward her and she backed away, confused. "Honey, I know it's fast, but what we're feeling is so natural. When I touch you I want—"

"No! Don't say it." She turned away from the obvious desire on his face. Staring out the window, she tried to calm her ragged breathing

"Why are you so shy with me? Haven't you ever gotten swept away like this before?" He was close behind her.

She shook her head, suddenly feeling young and inexperienced. The truth was that she'd never felt anything like this before, and it was scaring her to death.

He touched her shoulder and she flinched. "Don't, please," she whispered. "I don't want it to happen... I mean, I've never...." She trailed off, embarrassed and afraid of what he would think.

"Ah. I see." His voice behind her showed that he understood what she couldn't say. "I'm sorry, sweetheart. I guess I didn't realize..."

She turned and looked at him. "You're from a different world, and we really don't know each other very well. I don't know what happened just then, but—"

"But you don't think it's a good idea," he finished for her. "You're right, you're right." He ran his fingers through his hair, messing it up.

She couldn't think of anything to say. The intensity of his touch was too fresh in her mind, and she felt confused at the conflicting messages in her heart. Part of her wished he hadn't stopped.

He watched her, his breathing slowly returning to normal. Then he smiled and touched her lightly on the shoulder. "Hey, don't look so upset," he said. "I'm sorry if I was too... aggressive."

"It's okay. But I just can't..."

"I understand." He took a deep breath. "It's probably better this way. Because I'm only passing through, and I don't want to cause problems for you when I'm gone."

The words pierced her, erasing the last trace of excitement and pleasure that his kisses had created. She crossed her arms over her chest tightly.

"And," he said, "for the sake of my self-control, I guess I'll leave you alone now. Are we friends?"

She looked at him, feeling skeptical. "Well, for friends we disagree on a lot of things."

"But as my brother always says, we'll just agree to disagree."

"Sure," she said, and felt a stab in her heart as she watched him walk out the door.

Chapter Three

He was holding her, running his hands all over that tiny, rounded, oh-so-feminine body. Her dark hair fell across his face, its musky scent driving him wild, and he ran his hands slowly through it as she brought her ripe, full lips down softly on his—

"Boss! Hey, boss! There's trouble down at the site!"

With a start Cole Denton sat up in bed, breathing hard, sweat drenching his body. Dimly he recognized the hollering voice outside as belonging to one of his workers.

"I'll be right there," he called out as he climbed out of bed and automatically started putting on his clothes.

Remembering his dream, he swore softly. Lord, that woman was haunting him! He hadn't been far off when he'd called her a witch doctor; she had to be part witch to get under his skin so completely. He'd had the same dream more than once since the day, one week ago, when their kisses had aroused such unexpectedly strong passions between them. Each time the dream had ended before they'd had time to fulfill their desires.

You'd better find a different woman, he told himself. Skye Archer was too young, too innocent, and he knew the dangers of that sort of woman. Either he'd end up feeling guilty because he'd taken advantage of her, or he'd fall too hard and she'd leave him to test her wings with other men.

Like Deidre.

Impatiently he shook off the hurt feelings that still rose in him when he thought of her. She had wanted to experience the world, and he'd agreed with her; that was what she had needed to do. That she'd been tactless, that she'd been caught in a heated embrace with one of his workers...well, that could be attributed to her youth, too. He was mature enough to handle the embarrassment.

But the upshot was that he should stick to women his own age, for his own sake, and for the sake of the woman, too. And that meant leaving Skye Archer alone, despite the fact that his hormones and his dreams made it difficult to do.

That dream... Cole groaned when he realized the direction of his thoughts, and he slammed the door of his cabin hard as he headed for the site.

What he found there was sufficient to clear all other thoughts from his mind. All over the Denton equipment and on the side of the recreation center they were building, bright red spray-painted letters proclaimed a clear message.

Unsafe.

Save Our Kids—Get Rid of Denton Rec.

Denton Go Home.

Cole swore under his breath as he read the words and the various expletives that accompanied them. Clearly the local people were feeling a resurgence of anger toward Denton Recreation and what it was doing to their town. From the Save Our Kids remark, he knew that young Ricky Zale's injury on the site had been part of the stimulation for the new attack.

"What should we do, boss?" Stretch asked.

Looking around for the first time, Cole noticed that townspeople were gathering at the site, reading the words and commenting on them. The last thing he wanted was a lot of publicity that might arouse more bad feelings.

"Get the men started cleaning this up," he ordered. "Paint out the stuff on the equipment, and sand it off the building. Let's stop everything else until we've covered it." His fists clenched as he gave the order, mentally adding up the cost of the extra day's work.

Trying to moderate his anger, he approached the nearest group of townspeople. "Any ideas about who's responsible for this mess?" he asked them tightly.

The denials were quick—too quick, to Cole's finely attuned ear. The group dispersed, and he shook his head in frustration. Lord, these people stuck together.

He spotted Skye standing with Tom Zale and another man he'd seen around the village. They were talking intently. As he turned toward them, an unwelcome thought entered his mind.

Had Skye played any role in this vandalism? He remembered as clearly as if it were yesterday the words she'd said in anger at the hospital's emergency room. "That construction site is completely unsafe," she'd told him. He looked again at the words spray-painted on the equipment, and the coincidence was too close for comfort.

Resolutely he started over toward the group. The three of them grew silent as they watched his approach.

"Skye, do you know anything about this?" Cole asked.

Her eyes flew quickly to Tom, then back to meet his. "I don't know who did it, Cole," she said quickly.

"Any ideas?"

She hesitated and looked at the two men with her, but they were silent, watching her. "Look," she said finally, "whoever did this was pretty much expressing what everyone in town feels. We don't like what Denton Rec is doing to our way of life. And we don't like the fact that one of our kids was hurt here."

The two men looked approvingly at her, and Cole realized belatedly that the confrontation was a test of her loyalty. She'd been seen with him, and there was probably some speculation among her friends that she'd gone over to the side of the "enemy." But clearly, she hadn't.

"I feel rotten about the accident," he said, looking at the two men's closed faces and then turning back to Skye. "But the hole in the fence was fixed the day after that child got hurt, and I've done regular checks on the whole enclosure every day since then."

He thought he caught a spark of sympathy in her eyes, but her next words were resolute. "That's fine. But there are a lot of strangers here now. A lot of dust and trash, and Crooked Fork is starting to seem like a different town. People are hoping . . . well, that things like this—" she gestured at the garishly spray-painted wall of the new rec center "—will make you get out of town."

"Is that what you want, too?" The words felt wrenched out of him, and he regretted them immediately. Of course she couldn't show any positive feelings toward him in front of these men. And yet he felt an absurd urge to show them that he, too, had some sort of power over this beautiful girl they seemed so possessive about.

He was rewarded only by the sight of a faint blush creeping into her cheeks. "I don't much like the way our town is changing," she said. But her voice was gentle.

Cole turned to Tom Zale, who'd been silent during the whole exchange. "What about you, Zale?" he asked. "Any ideas about who's the artist here?"

The younger man's lip curled, and he ran a hand over his already smooth hair. "I don't know who's your painter. But like Skye said, we all would breathe easier if you'd take your big-time equipment somewhere else."

Cole sighed heavily. "Well, fine," he said. "I guess I didn't expect you folks to really tell me who painted up the equipment. But since I have no doubt at all that you know—" he raised a hand to stop Skye's immediate protest "—I'll leave a message with you to pass on to the vandals. The time my men spend cleaning off the spray paint is going to cost Denton Rec a good deal of money. And it's going to slow down our progress. That doesn't make me happy."

He paused for effect, and again he thought he saw a flash of sympathy in Skye's dark eyes. "If I have to post a guard, I will. If I have to bring the police in, I will. But nothing that you people do is going to get Denton out of here, because I'm not an outlaw to be run out of town. Got it?"

"Sure, we've got it," said Tom Zale, his lip curling again. "You talk big, old man. Wonder if you can back up the things you say?"

Cole's muscles flexed as he contemplated the younger man's insolent face. "Try me, Zale. Just try me." He turned abruptly and headed for the group of men painting out the sprayed-on words.

Skye arrived back at her cabin at noon, still shaken over what had been done to the construction site. She didn't blame Cole for his anger; the equipment was expensive, as was the time of his workers, so the vandalism was a real setback. She had her own suspicions about who had done the damage, and, much as she hated to admit it to herself, Tom Zale was among the possibilities in her mind. She'd asked him and he'd denied it, but she had seen the nervous way he'd responded to Cole's sharp questions.

Sighing, she walked out the cabin's back door and sat down on the oversized boulder that served as a bench. She hated what Denton Rec was doing to the village—the dirt and dust, the new people around town, and especially the vacationers who were starting to fill up the cottages that Denton had already completed. She didn't want the quiet mountain to change, but if Denton Rec's building projects continued, the old way of life would soon be gone. She hated the thought.

And yet the idea that Cole Denton might be forced to pack up and leave brought a pang to her heart. He'd looked so tired this morning, and so discouraged. With a flash of insight, she knew that there was a sensitive side to the man that had been hurt by the angry spray-painted slogans. He'd hidden the pain with his brusque words, but she'd sensed that it was there.

A flutter of wings in a nearby tree brought her mind back to the present. "Is that you, Kronos?" she said quietly, and made a clicking sound with her tongue.

For answer, a large crow swooped down to a branch beside her. The bird looked at her, its shiny black head cocked to one side.

"Oh, Kronos, I don't have anything for you right now," she said, laughing. The bird was a hopeless scavenger. She and Gran had found it several years ago on a forest path, chirping repeatedly for its mother, who was nowhere in sight. They'd fed it with an eyedropper and, miraculously, the tiny creature had lived. Now, although it had its freedom, the bird stuck close to the cabin.

"You know you've got it good here, don't you?" she asked. The bird hopped closer, and she could have sworn she saw expectancy in its beady eyes.

Grinning, she dug through her shirt pocket and found a candy bar wrapper she'd stuck in there that morning. She pulled it out, and at the sight of the shiny foil, the bird let out a squawk. Holding it so that the light bounced off the silver paper, she talked softly to the crow. After a moment's hesitation, it hopped onto her hand, grabbed the foil in its beak, and flew to the top of a nearby tree.

Skye laughed, then stood up and looked around. She needed to get some sketching done today. Her charcoal drawings were selling better than ever, and she could always use the extra money.

She loved to draw, but she hated the thought of being cooped up inside the cabin this afternoon. Maybe she could bring her sketch pad outside to work. Her mind made up, she went inside to get her equipment.

When she couldn't see her sketch pad clearly anymore, she looked up at the sky. No wonder! Dark, forbidding clouds hung dangerously low, and the tiny bright spot that marked the sun's location was far to the west.

She'd worked all day, as she often did, without realizing how quickly time was passing.

As she put her gear away, she heard a car stop in her driveway, and moments later a knock sounded at the door. She paused, puzzled. Who would have come up the mountain this far when the weather looked so forbidding? But it had to be someone she knew; Farimer hadn't barked at all.

She opened the door to see Cole Denton's tall form before her.

"Hi," she said. "I'm surprised to see you here."

"Can I come in? It's getting chilly."

She opened the door wider in invitation. "Can I get you some hot coffee or tea?"

"Hot tea sounds great," he said, rubbing his hands together. Skye noticed that they were rough and reddened.

He sat silently at the table as Skye moved around the kitchen. While she waited for the kettle to boil, she heated up some leftover vegetable soup and sliced bread and cheese onto a platter.

"I haven't had lunch or dinner, and I'm starving," she said by way of explanation as she brought the tray of food to the table. "Help yourself."

Conversation was scanty as they ate, and Skye found herself stealing frequent glances at Cole. His eyes had dark circles under them, and his shoulders were slumped slightly, but he ate the soup and sandwiches with enthusiasm.

"This is great," he said finally as he leaned back in his chair. His eyes had taken on a trace of their former twinkle, and his work-roughened hands rested contentedly on his stomach. "It sure does beat soup from a can."

His satisfied voice made her smile. "I'm glad you liked it," she said. "I love to cook—and to eat." She rose and started to clear the stoneware dishes from the table.

"Let me help you wash up," he said, bringing his own dishes to the sink. They worked together quietly, and within a few minutes the supper was cleared away.

Skye opened a bottle of homemade wine that Pop Jones had given her when she'd brought him the liniment the previous week. "This stuff may be pretty powerful," she warned as she handed Cole a glass. They moved into the living room and sank down in front of the fireplace.

"You know, you're a comfortable person," he said.

"What do you mean?"

"You don't ask a lot of questions," he explained. "Like tonight. I come in uninvited and unexpected, and you don't stand there and ask me my business. You give me dinner and make me feel right at home."

She flushed at the compliment. "That's country hospitality, I guess," she said lightly. "But I have to admit, I am curious...."

"About why I came?"

She nodded. "I would have thought that I was the last person you'd want to see after what happened at the site this morning."

A muscle twitched in his cheek. "I wasn't that happy with anyone earlier today, it's true. We spent almost all day painting that stuff out and scraping the rec center's wall. What a waste of time."

She looked at the floor, studying one of the knots in the wood. She felt bad for him, but she didn't want to be disloyal to her friends and neighbors. And she certainly understood the sentiment that had made them paint the ugly words all over the site, even though her own feelings would never have taken such an outlet.

"What's so terrible about Denton Rec coming into this place, Skye?" he asked. "That's the real question I wanted to ask you tonight. I know we're changing some things, and there are new people coming in. I can understand some resentment. But this place is in bad shape economically, and Denton will offer a lot of new jobs for people."

"We haven't seen any Help Wanted signs around."

"Well, that takes time. We have to get the place started, get things built. We need skilled workers during these first stages. But once the recreation area gets going, there will be jobs for probably half of the working people in the area, if they want them."

She frowned. "No one realizes that, I guess. I didn't. All we see is that there are a lot of strangers around. Snobbish tourists in fancy clothes, who come up and walk around the settlement and talk about how quaint it all is." Her voice grew mocking. "Look, Mildred! That child's barefoot, and it's only forty degrees out! Look, Beverly! That girl's no more than nineteen and she has three children already. Aren't they *interesting* people!"

Cole flinched. "Is it that bad?"

"Yes! Not to mention the men that gawk at the women as if they were on display."

He sighed. "Look, I can see why that bothers you. But to be honest, you people are a little unusual. It hardly seems like the twentieth century here."

The stick she'd been fiddling with snapped abruptly as her head jerked up. "When I lived in Denver, I got a healthy dose of the twentieth century," she said. "And I didn't much like it. People didn't know the names of their neighbors. You couldn't even open your door at night for fear the person knocking was a criminal maniac. The noise never stopped, and people with breathing problems had to stay indoors half the time because of all the air pollution."

"I never thought about the city in quite that way."

"I hated it," she said. "I was never so happy as when I came back and saw all the people here. People I'd known all my life and knew I could trust. And the air was so fresh...." She breathed appreciatively, remembering the feeling.

"That it is," he said, smiling at her. "But there are some things about this place that really drive me nuts."

"Like what?"

"People are so closed. In their minds, in their ways of looking at things. I've never felt such animosity as I feel here. It's hard to take."

"It must be lonely for you," she said. Then she wondered if it was her business to tell this big-city businessman about how lonely he was.

He reached out and put a finger under her chin, making her eyes meet his. "It is lonely. That's the other reason I came up here, in fact." He grinned at her. "I was awfully sick of eating TV dinners alone in my cabin."

"You came looking for dinner!"

"Well, sort of. That, and the company of a beautiful, compassionate woman."

She felt the color rush into her cheeks and pulled away from him, staring across the room. Her heart was pounding faster. "Why else did you come?"

"Isn't that reason enough?" He laughed at the embarrassment in her flushed face. "But actually, there is another reason. I want you to do me a favor."

Her eyebrows rose as she waited to hear it.

"I want you to find a way to give this to Ricky Zale's mother." He pulled a wad of bills from his pocket and handed them to her.

She stared at the thick roll of twenties. "Why...?"

"I went to the settlement yesterday to see how the kid was doing. Denton Rec is covering the hospital costs, of course, but I wanted to see for myself that the boy was okay."

She nodded, waiting.

"They wouldn't let me in."

"Who wouldn't?"

"Your friend Tom, and Ricky's mother. I think she would have talked to me if Tom hadn't been there telling her I was the one who'd caused Ricky's accident."

She frowned. Tom was her friend; she'd known him all her life. But she knew he had a hot temper and tended to hold grudges.

"I did see, before Tom ordered me off the property with a shotgun, that they're in pretty bad shape financially," Cole said. "The place looked really run-down. I figured on giving them something to help out, but I know they'd never take it from me directly."

"So you want me to give this to them?"

"To Ricky's mother," he nodded. "Some way that she won't feel bad about taking it. But don't give it to your friend Tom." His voice sounded bitter as he mentioned the man's name.

She put her hand on his arm hesitantly. "That's nice of you. And I'm sorry about Tom. He's... well, he's pretty close-minded about people."

"Is he your boyfriend?"

Her head shot up at the abrupt question. "Sort of," she admitted.

"What does that mean? How can you have a 'sort of' boyfriend?"

She shrugged. The intent look in his eyes was making her uncomfortable. "Everyone at the settlement expects us to get married," she said.

"Are you going to?"

"I don't know."

"How do you feel about him?"

"He's an old friend. I care about him."

"He's a jerk!" Abruptly Cole rose and paced across the room. He stared unseeingly out the window.

"Don't say that about him."

He turned back to her, his eyes flaming. "Why not? Does it hurt you? Are you so in love with him that you're blind to his faults?"

"No! I know he has faults. So does everyone."

"Well, then, does he excite you? Do you like it when he kisses you?"

"That's none of your business!" She stood and turned away from him angrily. She didn't want to think about the way that Cole's kisses last week had moved her far more than Tom's ever had.

"Hey, I shouldn't have asked you that," he said. His voice was nearer than she'd expected, and she turned toward it, then hesitated. He was standing right next to her, and the way he was looking at her caused a tremor deep within. Was it fear? Or excitement?

"It's okay," she said, looking down at the floor. But the shakiness of her voice made her emotional turmoil plain.

"Look at me, Skye." He grasped her shoulders and she raised her eyes to meet his. Their gray color seemed to have deepened, and she heard his breathing rasp in the quiet cabin. "Oh, Lord. I can't help myself."

His lips descended onto hers as he drew her into his arms. He kissed her tenderly at first, gently, and without demand. But she sensed in the tightness of his body, the effort his restraint required.

In a moment she turned away. "Please don't start this, Cole," she whispered.

"Why not?" His breath was warm against her cheek. "I just want to hold you for a while. It's nothing to be afraid of." His arms tightened almost imperceptibly around her.

She met his eyes, and saw the warmth there. His arms around her were strong and comforting. Yet she feared where it might lead, and she knew that Cole wouldn't be around to deal with the consequences.

"I don't think we should..."

"Then don't think. Just feel." He touched her cheek, his finger as gentle as if she were made of glass. Softly, lightly, his thumb brushed her lower lip. "You have such beautiful lips. They're so full, so sweet. So inviting." His mouth moved to the place his thumb had brushed as his fingers tangled in her hair.

The warmth spread through Skye's body as she allowed herself to be drawn in by his soothing words and skillful hands. The rest of the world melted away as she felt him suck gently at her lower lip. Her heart pounded harder.

"I love your hair," he whispered against her ear. "So long and thick. Like an Indian's." He pulled long strands up over her shoulders and let them fall across her breasts. "I'd like to see you with nothing but your hair to cover you."

She drew in her breath sharply and tried to pull away. "No, Cole. We can't do this."

"Just for a minute more," he said. He stroked her back, up and down, in a soothing rhythm as he brushed light kisses all over her face.

Shuddering, she closed her eyes tightly. His lips were soft, but there was a roughness to his face that told her he hadn't shaved that morning. The contrast in sensations made her breathing quicken.

His lips took hers, more passionately this time. She felt the tip of his tongue invade her, probing tentatively, and her lips opened for him almost of their own accord. Her mind reeled and she clung to him, feeling the hardness of his muscles under the thin work shirt.

As he felt her response, his arms tightened around her, his hands moving harder on her back to draw her in. His motions strained the material of her shirt against her swelling breasts, and she gasped.

"You're not wearing a bra, are you?" he asked as his hands traced patterns on her back.

"No," she whispered.

He held her away from him, and his eyes swept slowly down her body, taking in the tautened fabric of her blouse. "I like that," he said softly.

The heat rose in her cheeks, and her breathing grew shallow and fast under his gaze. "Cole..."

"I'm just saying what I feel, honey," he said. He drew her back against his chest and stroked her hair. "You know what I'd like to do, don't you?"

She heard his heart's pounding as she rested her face against his broad chest. "I think so," she whispered.

"What do you think about it?" His hands were gentle as they stroked her, but the hardness of his body told her how anxiously he waited for her answer.

She twisted in his arms to look up at him. "I'm—I'm scared," she told him. "I've never felt this way before. I like it, but . . ."

"But what?"

"What will I do when you're gone?"

The plaintive question hung in the air between them in the cabin's silence. Cole's jaw tightened as he looked down at her, and she saw the warmth flare up in his eyes before he spoke.

"You're wise, Skye." Firmly he put her away from him. "And I should go home." In a smooth movement he strode across the cabin, his back rigid.

Hastily she straightened her clothes. The spell was broken, and she felt an ache of loneliness at the thought that he would leave now.

A glimpse at the clock on the mantle startled her. "It's ten o'clock already!" she said in surprise.

"Time flies when you're having . . ." He trailed off as he turned to grin at her. "Sorry. Stupid joke."

"What's it like outside?" She pressed her face against the window, peering out into the darkness. To her shock, a blanket of white coated the trees and ground. "Oh, no, Cole. Look at this."

"What the devil . . ." he said as he came up behind her and peered out. "It's the end of May! How can there be snow on the ground?"

"You're in the mountains," she said, chuckling. "We've had snow in June before."

"I wonder how deep it is." He strode across the room and threw the front door open. Gingerly he stepped out. "About four inches, and it's coming down hard," he called back to her.

"You'll have to stay the night."

"What?" He came back inside, a puzzled expression on his face.

"I said, you'll have to stay the night. You can't drive down the mountain in this."

"Sure I can."

She rolled her eyes. "Oh, for heaven's sake. Don't be stupid and macho. No one from around here would ever try to drive that road in a snowstorm, and you're not even familiar with the area. Forget it."

He eyed her narrowly for a moment, then shrugged. "If you say so. But leaving was going to be my main tool of self-control."

She laughed. "Oh, no, you don't. You're not going to use the storm as an excuse for bad behavior. I'll expect you to do your share of the work around here, and that will keep your mind on the straight and narrow."

"Work?" he asked in mock horror.

She nodded. "For starters," she said, hands on hips, "you can bring in a couple of loads of wood. It's getting downright cold in here."

He groaned. "Slave driver. Where is it?"

As she directed him to the woodpile outside the cabin's back door, she found herself grinning. Why did she feel so lighthearted, so happy? It was often lonely up here, and she had always liked to have company. But the warmth generated by Cole's presence went beyond anything she was used to.

She walked into her bedroom and shivered. It wasn't nearly as well insulated as the rest of the house, and on cold nights it was almost uninhabitable. Normally, on such nights, she slept by the fire. Smiling to herself, she remembered how cozy those nights had been during her childhood. She, Gran, and Gramps had often brought bedrolls out by the stove, and inevitably they'd ended up talking long into the dark nights.

Cole appeared at the bedroom door. "Where do I sleep? In here?" He walked in and looked around. "Hey, it's freezing in here."

"I know. I usually sleep by the fire on cold nights."

"Great idea. It sounds romantic."

"That's exactly what I'm afraid of."

He put an arm across her shoulders. "I'll try to be good," he said. Then he caught sight of the large bookshelf that lined the bedroom's far wall. "See, I'll just grab one of these books and improve my mind for a while before going to sleep."

He scanned the titles casually at first, and then with increasing interest. "Hey, you've got some great stuff here. Do you read a lot?"

"All the time."

"What are your favorites?"

She approached the shelves. "This," she said, pulling out a thick volume. "And this. And this."

"*Emma*, Homer's *Odyssey*, and *One Hundred Great Mystery Tales*," he read from the books' bindings. "That's a pretty broad range."

She laughed. "Actually I love almost all of these books. They belonged to Gramps, mostly, and we both always read a lot in the evenings. No TV up here, you know."

"How come you lived with your grandparents instead of your parents?" he asked as they left the freezing room.

"My parents died when I was a baby."

"Do you mind if I ask . . ."

"Not at all." She squatted down by the fire and stared into it absently. "When I was born, my father decided that we should leave the mountain. Even back then, it was tough to make a living here."

He sank down beside her, nodding.

"So we moved to San Francisco. They left me with a baby-sitter one night about six months after they'd arrived there." She paused. It did hurt to think about it, even though it had been so long ago. "They were both killed by a drunk driver, and Gran came out and got me."

"I'm sorry."

She smiled briefly at him. "Gran and Gramps were great parents to me. They were always young at heart."

"I'll bet you miss them."

She nodded. "That's the worst thing about being raised by grandparents. You get left alone younger."

Cole leaned toward her and caught her chin in his hand. "Are you lonely, Skye?"

She met his eyes, and their intensity enveloped her. Unable to pretend indifference to him, she nodded. "Yes, I'm lonely sometimes," she admitted.

"Are you glad I'm staying here tonight?" His voice was low and vibrant, and he continued to stroke her face gently with one finger.

She studied the knob on the old Franklin stove. "It feels good to have someone to talk to."

"Is that all you feel for me? Glad to have someone to talk to?"

She caught his hand and pulled it away from her face. "What are you trying to do, Cole?" she asked. "What do you want me to say? That I liked it when you held me? That your kisses make me feel different than I ever felt before?"

"Is that true?"

She still studied the stove's knob, unwilling to meet his eyes. "You know it is," she whispered.

"But you still don't want it to go any further."

She looked at his hands as they rolled and unrolled the edge of his now-untucked work shirt. They were strong hands, working hands, and the sight of them made her remember the tender way he'd touched her. Her heart started to thud harder. But she had to resist her desire for the warmth and tenderness Cole had to offer. Because he wouldn't be there forever; in fact, he'd be gone before summer's end.

"Skye?"

"I'll go get the bedding," she said, ignoring the question in his voice. She felt completely off-balance because of this man. She should hate him, or at least dislike him, because he stood for Denton Recreation and thus for all the unwanted changes happening in the village. But instead she felt drawn to him. Nothing seemed so appealing to her as to curl up in his arms and talk the night away with him.

After she pulled the quilts off her bed, she stood still for a moment and closed her eyes. She had to get herself under control. Letting Cole get too close to her would be a major mistake—one she could ill afford.

With a sigh she carried the heavy quilts out to the fireplace. Cole lay propped up on one elbow in front of it, casually perusing the book of mystery stories. Ignoring him, she folded the quilts into thick pads and lay them down on opposite sides of the stove. Then she tucked extra sheets and quilts over the tops of the pads.

"So far apart?" His question was only half teasing.

She nodded without smiling. "Do you want me to leave the lights on so you can read? Or are you ready to sleep?"

"You can turn them off," he said, sighing.

Only the flickering firelight illuminated the cabin once she'd switched off the two lamps. She slipped halfway into her pallet, then hastily slid out of her skirt and shirt. She'd brought out her nightshirt, an old work shirt that had belonged to Gramps, and she quickly pulled it on.

As she buttoned up the shirtfront, she heard a zipper going down, and stiffened. She hadn't considered how tense it would be to be so lightly clothed and sleeping in the same room with Cole. Forcing her mind away from the sound of him removing his clothes, she slid down into the covers.

An hour later she still hadn't fallen asleep. She couldn't tell whether Cole had, either. The thought of his nearness was just too disturbing, and she couldn't stop thinking about the way his kisses had made her feel.

"Are you asleep?" he asked in a quiet whisper.

"No," she said.

"Why don't you talk to me then? Since we're both sleepless."

Her eyes wide open, she stared up into the darkness. The sound of his voice was a comfort, making the night seem cozy rather than lonely. "What should we talk about?" she asked.

"Tell me about why you run down the mountain every week and men chase you."

She flopped over onto her stomach and raised herself up onto her elbows. "You wouldn't understand that."

"Try me."

Something about the night and his soft, gentle voice reassured her. "Okay. It's tradition," she explained. "The women in this family have always done it, ever since Gran's mother and father built this cabin way up here."

"What's the point of it?"

"You're not going to believe it," she said. "The man that catches you gets to marry you."

She heard his bedclothes rustle. "What?"

"If a man catches you, he gets to marry you."

"That's ridiculous!"

She rolled over onto her back. "See, I told you you wouldn't understand."

"Of course I don't understand. It's completely primitive! Like a courtship ritual among tribal people, or something."

"Please don't put it down, Cole," she said, her voice low. "I know it's strange. But there's a certain amount of logic there."

"What logic?"

She sat up, wrapping her arms around her knees. "Well, if a man could catch me, it would mean that he was very strong and fast. And smart."

"Why smart?"

"Because he'd have to know the mountain," she explained. "He'd have to know how to avoid snakes, and cactus plants, and all the other dangers—just like I do."

"I see," he said. "But why is that important?"

"Because," she said patiently, "a man who was smart, as well as fast and strong, would probably be a good husband and father for my children."

She could tell from his voice that he'd sat up, too. "But what if you didn't even like him?"

"That would be a problem," she said, chuckling. "But it doesn't seem to happen that way. At least for Gran and Mom, the men who caught them were men they ended up loving a lot."

He shook his head, a low whistle coming from his throat. "This culture seems more and more strange to me," he said. "So you're really going to marry the man who catches you running down that mountain? In this day and age?"

She was silent for a moment, thinking. "I suppose I'd have to," she said. "But it's not likely to happen. No one's caught me yet. And I don't know how long I'll go on playing the game."

"What about Zale?"

"He can't catch me."

Suddenly his voice took on a low, dangerous quality. "What would happen if someone from outside the settlement caught you?"

"I . . . I don't know. I never thought about it."

"I'll bet I could catch you."

She laughed out loud. "You couldn't."

"I could."

She flopped back down onto her back. "You're an outsider, Cole. It wouldn't be...well, it just wouldn't be right for you to do things our way. You don't take the tradition seriously."

"Do you?"

"To a certain extent, yes. And I don't want to talk about it anymore."

"Why?"

"Because I think you're laughing at me, I think you're just like those tourists who talk about how quaint we are. And I don't like it."

She heard him rustling again, and then the sound of something being pushed across the floor. "What are you doing?" she asked, alarmed.

"I'm coming over there." He was only dimly visible in the dark, sliding his pallet closer to hers.

"Wait just a—"

"There, now," he said when he'd pushed the bedding to within a few inches of hers. He slid inside. "This is better."

"I'm not so sure..."

He reached over and put one hand gently on her shoulder. "I want to be able to see you a bit," he said. "And I wasn't laughing at you. It's just that... you're different from the other people here. It seems a shame for you to be caught up in their ways."

"There's nothing wrong with their ways. Those are my ways, too." Her body had gone rigid as she stared up into the darkness, not looking his way.

His hand was stroking her shoulder now, ever so gently. "I'm sorry, Skye. I don't want to insult you."

"An outsider can't understand."

"Hey." He scooted over until his face was propped on an elbow directly beside her. "Don't shut me out like everyone else has."

"It's dangerous to let you get close to me!"

"Why, sweetheart? Why are you afraid?"

She turned her back to him and lay curled up on her side. "Just because," she mumbled. How could she tell him that she didn't want him to go? That if he got her started thinking about the outside world and then left, she'd never be content here again?

She heard him sigh deeply behind her. Then, before she could protest, he had gathered her into his arms, curled spoonlike behind her.

"Stop it, Cole! What are you—"

"Ssh. Just relax." His voice was soft and silky in her ear, his arms comforting around her. "I just want to hold you a minute. I won't start anything."

She lay, tense and stiff, locked in his grasp. It felt too good, too tempting, this having his arms around her.

"Just rest, honey. You're okay. Everything's going to be fine." He gently kissed the top of her head and then lay still, holding her.

Slowly, by degrees, she let her body relax against him. The thick quilts provided a kindly barrier, allowing the warmth of him to penetrate her. Their differences faded from her mind as she slipped drowsily into a doze.

Dimly she was aware of him stroking her hair, and she felt more kisses planted on the top of her head. She snuggled back against the warm presence behind her and drifted further into sleep.

Chapter Four

Skye, honey. Wake up. There's someone here."

The whispered words brought her slowly, reluctantly, out of the cozy world of sleep. "What . . . what's going on?" she asked, confused.

"There's someone here. At the door."

As the words sank in, she jackknifed into a sitting position, her eyes springing open. "It's bright in here!" she said.

"I think we overslept."

The pounding at the door pierced her consciousness. "Just a minute," she yelled. She kicked off the tangled quilts and stood up, then blushed as she saw Cole's smoldering glance. Her long legs were bare, and the thin nightshirt didn't hide her figure very well. He, she noticed, was fully dressed.

Hurriedly she reached for the skirt and blouse she'd shed the night before. "Could you turn around, please?" she asked, still blushing at the look in his eyes.

"If I have to."

The pounding started up again as she finished buttoning the blouse. "Coming!" she called impatiently as she ran across the floor to the cabin's front door.

She flung the door open. The beauty of the crystal-white world outside was lost on her as she recognized the man whose hand was raised to pound again. "Tom! What—"

"I just came up to see if you were all right. That storm was pretty unexpected."

"Thanks," she said weakly.

"Well, can I come in?" He was already stamping the snow off his boots.

"Uh, sure. Of course." She held the door open for him, groaning inwardly.

"Boy, that sure was a storm last night. Almost a foot. 'Course, it'll melt off fast. It's already warming up." He had finished taking off his jacket and had hung it on the hook by the door with easy familiarity. Now he turned.

"I see you slept by the fire—" His voice broke off abruptly as he took in the double pallet and then Cole's form in the rocking chair. "You!" he said in a low, shocked voice.

"Hello, Zale," Cole said lazily.

Tom was silent for a long moment as he looked from one to the other. His face flushed brick red.

"Tom, it's not what you—"

"I can see damn well what it is." His voice was low and furious.

"The snowstorm came and Cole was—"

"I didn't think you were that kind of woman."

Skye flinched at his tone. "I'm not any kind of woman. I'm me."

"But you're not the same." Tom grabbed his coat and yanked the door open. Then he turned back to look at Cole with an expression that was pure poison.

"Tom, wait..."

"Forget it." He slammed out.

She ran out after him, oblivious to the snow on her bare feet. The disappointment and betrayal in his voice were too much for her to bear, even though she knew he had no real right to feel those things about her. She'd never made any kind of commitment to him, but she hadn't been firm in discouraging his deepening feelings.

"Please, Tom, wait. It isn't true. He got snowed in here, that's all. He never... we never..."

"Do you think I'm stupid enough to believe that?" he flung back over his shoulder.

"Tom, look at me."

Finally he stopped and turned. "I could strangle you for what you've done."

"It's not what you think. You have to believe me."

He gripped her hard by the shoulders and looked into her eyes. "You're not Denton's woman?"

She shook her head. "No, Tom. I'm not."

After a moment he shoved her gently away. "You'd best get inside," he said, his voice gruff. "You'll catch cold."

"Do you believe me?"

"I don't know." He turned away from her and walked a few steps, then paused. "Do you still want me to come for dinner tonight? Or are you busy?"

She knew his opinion of her would hinge on her answer. "Of course I want you to come, Tom. I've been planning on it. I'm going to make your favorite stew."

He grunted and tramped off down the path, not looking back. She watched him a moment, then turned back to the cabin.

Cole stood at the open door, his arms crossed in front of his chest. His lips were pressed in a tight line. "Well, did you convince him of your purity?" he asked.

"I don't know," she said, sidling past him to get inside. She grabbed a towel and started rubbing her cold, pink feet. "I sure hope so."

He squatted down in front of her. "Why is it so important to you that Zale should believe in your...innocence? Why is that important enough that you'd run out barefooted in the snow to convince him?" His voice was harsh and angry.

"You wouldn't understand."

He snatched the towel from her and started rubbing her feet roughly. "Don't pull that on me again! I have to know!" His voice lowered. "Is it because you love him?"

She hesitated, wondering what the emotion in his voice meant. "No. It's not that," she said.

"Then what?"

She sighed and stood up, pacing restlessly across the floor. "If Tom thought I'd slept with you, then the whole settlement would find out. He'd be so mad, he'd go yelling about it to everyone. And that would be awful."

"Don't tell me all of the women here are virgins until they marry. That's hard to believe in this day and age."

"No, not all are," she said, shaking her head. "The truth is, it's because you're an outsider. And not only an outsider, but the person who's behind the whole Denton Recreation thing."

"So what would happen if they thought you'd spent the night with me? Which you did, of course."

She flushed. "If they thought we were lovers, I'd be shunned. People might never trust me again."

"So in any match, you'll take their side, eh? Not mine?"

"They're my people, Cole," she said softly. "They'll always be here. You won't."

His jaw tightened. "I see," he said. Then he walked to their pallets and started folding up the quilts.

"I can do that."

"Just want me out of here as soon as possible, do you?"

"No! I didn't mean that at all." She frowned. She had only spoken the truth about his eventual departure, and he hadn't contradicted her. So why did he seem so angry? And why did she feel so devastated?

His movements were quick and jerky as he gathered his things together. "Thanks for the shelter," he said, and turned toward the door.

"Cole..."

He turned back, waiting. Their eyes met for a long moment, but there was none of the instant communication they'd shared last night.

"Never mind," she said.

"See you around, then." He slammed out the door.

Ignoring the pile of bedding, Skye sank down into her rocking chair. What a mess. Tom was going to be suspicious of her now, and she still feared that word of Cole's nighttime visit would spread around the settlement. But worse was the ache that her quarrel with Cole had created inside her. She'd thought that if she could keep him at bay physically, emotional closeness wouldn't be a problem.

But she hadn't quite kept him at bay, she reminded herself. The memory of his arms around her in the night made a warm tingle spread through her body. She vaguely remembered him whispering tender words to her as she'd slept in his arms, and the hands that had stroked her hair had been as comforting as Gran's had been when she was a child.

Abruptly she stood up. She couldn't dwell on those moments. Cole would be gone soon enough, and she ought not to build up a store of memories that would only haunt her later.

Later in the afternoon, as she chopped onions for stew, she felt a tautness in her stomach that wouldn't go away. She was scared, plain scared, of what Tom had decided. He had softened toward her when she had run after him that morning, but when he reflected on what he'd seen, she knew the evidence would seem damning.

The fumes from the onion made her eyes water, but she continued relentlessly. As the cleaver flashed up and down, she worried about what conclusions he'd finally decided to draw. She had run down to the settlement to see Lyn earlier in the afternoon, and her friend had known something was bothering him.

"What's wrong with him, Skye?" she'd asked. "He seemed so mad, or something. But he said he was going up to your place for dinner."

She had shrugged off the question and made a quick excuse to leave. But Lyn's statement had only added to her worry.

Her thoughts turned to the questions Cole had been asking the night before. Would she marry Tom if he caught her? Would she marry him, anyway? She'd always considered it a real possibility; he was the only man in the settlement who interested her at all, and their shared childhood memories made a strong bond between them.

But now the thought of sharing a bed and a life with Tom was far less appealing. She suspected that he knew something about the sabotage at Cole's site, and she knew, too, that he was dead-set against any sort of change in the mountain life-style. To marry him would mean that she'd have to support him in his bitter fight against progress of any kind, and she didn't believe in him fully enough to do that.

But mainly, she didn't love Tom in the way a woman should love her husband. The warmth, the passion she had felt with Cole had convinced her of that.

She'd have to make her position clear tonight, she realized, and her stomach twisted with nervousness. It simply wasn't fair to let him think she had stronger feelings than she did.

Her nervousness hadn't gone away by the time she heard Tom's knock on the cabin door, and she slowly walked to the door and pulled it open.

Tom's brusqueness did nothing to calm her nerves, and by the time they'd finished dinner she felt drawn tight enough to snap.

"Can I get you a drink?" she asked him when she'd finished clearing their dishes away.

He still hadn't moved from the dinner table. He didn't, in fact, even seem to hear her.

"Tom? A drink?"

He turned to her with a start. "Sure, hon. Scotch would be great."

She brought their drinks to the sitting area where Tom had drawn up a chair by the fire. He took his with a grunt, which she assumed was supposed to stand for "thank you."

Suddenly she was tired of his unwillingness to communicate. She tapped his knee to get his attention. "Are you trying to punish me for what you saw this morning, by not talking to me?"

He frowned, but at least she'd got his full attention now. "You've got to expect me to be upset about it," he said.

"Don't you believe me when I say that nothing happened between us?"

He took a long draw on his drink. "It's a little hard to believe, Skye," he said. "I know that man wants you. It's plain in his eyes. And I saw how all your bedding was tangled up together on the floor." The last words seemed almost choked out of him, and the pain in his dark eyes was obvious.

She was silent, thinking guiltily of the way Cole had held her in the night.

As if he had read her thoughts, Tom leaned toward her and met her eyes. "I'll take your word on the fact that the two of you aren't lovers—yet. I don't believe you'd lie to me about that. But can you honestly say that Denton didn't touch you at all last night?"

She turned away from his gaze and stared unseeingly across the room. She could feel the hot blood rising in her cheeks.

"So he did touch you."

She couldn't answer him, but the guilty look on her face was all the proof he needed.

"Dammit, Skye," he said, his voice thick with frustration. "I've always thought of you as belonging to me. You're the only woman I've ever loved."

Something twisted inside of her as she saw the pain on Tom's familiar face. But she had to tell him the truth; no matter how much it hurt him now, the pain would be worse if she waited until later.

"Tom, I don't think I'm the right woman for you," she said.

"I know you're the right woman for me."

"No, I'm not."

"What you mean is, I'm not the right man for you," he said. "Isn't that right?"

She looked steadily at the floor, her hands pleating the hem of her dress accordion fashion. "I care about you, Tom. I always have—"

The scrape of his chair across the hardwood floor was harsh as he rose abruptly. "Don't try to soften the blow! I can tell what you mean, and it hurts worse that you're treating me like a kid who can be comforted with a few soft words."

"Oh, Tom. I'm so sorry."

"Damn that Cole Denton. If he hadn't come..."

"We still wouldn't have been right for each other."

He stared at her for a moment, and the hurt in his eyes was plain. She felt her stomach twist as she saw the slump in his shoulders. As if it required a major effort to get the words out, he spoke. "Skye, you know that he'll be gone soon. And he won't take you with him. Couldn't we just...hang on until then? And try again?"

Slowly she shook her head. "I don't think so," she said.

"Maybe I didn't try hard enough with you." He ran a hand distractedly over his hair. "I always tried not to come on too strong so as not to scare you off. I thought we had all the time in the world. But I guess I should have made my move on you sooner."

She stiffened as he approached her. "Please, I don't—"

He held out his arms to her. "Come on, honey. Just let me kiss you and hold you one last time."

Reluctantly she rose from her chair. He pulled her close to him, tangling his fingers in her hair. His kiss was hard and searching.

The feeling wasn't unpleasant, but neither did it make her dizzy and weak as Cole's drugging kisses had done. After a moment, when she was sure of her own feelings, she tried to pull away.

"Please, Skye. Don't hold back from me now. You taste so sweet." His murmuring voice held a hint of desperation.

When his hand came up to cup her breast, she pushed him harder and twisted her face away. "Stop it, Tom! That's enough!"

But his arms remained locked around her, and for a horrifying moment she had to endure his searching hand and increasingly passionate kisses.

"No! Stop it now!" With a gathering of strength, she managed to break away from him. Her whole body shaking, she stepped quickly away. "You'd better go home now," she said.

His breathing was hard and labored as he looked at her, frustration plain on his face. "I'm sorry, Skye. But I know I could make you happy if you'd only let me..."

"No!"

His lip curled slightly. "All right, if that's the way you want it. You can have Denton. But no one at the settlement's going to think much of your choice."

"Just because I choose not to have you doesn't mean that I want him!"

"Come off it. I know exactly why you've gone so cold on me now, all of a sudden." He grabbed his coat off the hook by the door, then turned to her. As he looked at her quietly, the anger drained out of his face. "I guess I won't be chasing you down the mountain anymore," he said softly.

"It was about time for me to stop playing that game, anyway. By the time Mom and Gran were my age, they were already married."

He stared at her for a long moment. Then he reached into his pocket and pulled out his wallet. Fumbling through it, he extracted a picture. "Here. I guess I won't be needing this now."

She took the picture he held out to her and looked at it. Worn and cracked, but still recognizable, it showed her and Tom as children, running down the mountain together. They were hand in hand, their faces full of childish joy.

"I always thought to show that to our kids one day," he said. Then he was out the door. She ran to the window and watched as he trudged, shoulders slumped, down the path. Just before he got to the edge of the forest, he stopped and turned. For a long moment he stared back at the cabin. Then, head bent, he turned and disappeared into the trees.

When he was out of sight Skye turned and walked unseeingly across the cabin. She sank down into her rocking chair and drew her knees up. Her fingers smoothed out the old photograph repeatedly, rhythmically, as she rocked.

It was only when she realized that her tears were falling onto the photograph that she set it aside.

Chapter Five

Quit trying to be perfect!"

"I'm not trying to be perfect!"

"You are, too!"

Skye's sharp reply died on her lips. Ruefully she surveyed her friend. "Well, maybe I am, at that."

Laboriously, Lyn lowered herself into the easy chair, hands supporting her weight on the chair's arms. "I knew I could knock some sense into you if I kept hammering away at it," she said. "Skye, you've tried to please the people in this settlement every day of your life. It's time you paid some attention to your own feelings."

"But I can't figure them out!"

"Well, I can," Lyn said, shifting her weight into a more comfortable position. Her pregnancy seemed much farther advanced than the last time Skye had seen her, and she was definitely at the uncomfortable stage now.

Still, she was as shrewd about her friend as ever. "I know for a fact that you're attracted to Cole Denton," she said. "It shows plain as day every time you talk about him. And I say you should let it happen."

"But he's Denton Rec! Everyone here hates him!"

"I don't think he's that bad, really. Did you know that Bob got a job working for him?"

Skye leaned forward in surprise. "You're kidding!"

The blond woman shook her head. "No. Mr. Denton put up a sign last week saying he needed workers. And I made Bob go and apply." She paused and patted her swollen belly. "He didn't want to at first. You know, he thought everyone would be upset with him for working down at the site. But with the baby due any minute, we really need the money."

"How does he like it?"

"He says it's a good job. He's working hard—Mr. Denton makes sure of that. But he's a fair boss. One day Bob was late for work because I was feeling so bad that he had to get the kids up and bathed and take them over to Mom's." She paused, frowning. "I thought he'd lose the job for sure, since it was his first week and all. But when he explained to Mr. Denton what had happened, he was real nice about it. Even told Bob to take a long lunch hour and come up to check on me."

"Really?"

Lyn nodded. "Some of the folks still hate Denton Rec. But I'm glad they're here, now. It looks like Bob may have a permanent job, finally, and we'll be able to stay on the mountain."

Skye studied her teacup thoughtfully. So Cole had put up a Help Wanted sign after all! She wondered briefly whether her own suggestion to that effect had had anything to with his decision. She hadn't seen Cole for over a week, ever since the night he'd gotten snowed in at her cabin and they'd parted in anger. For all she knew, he could still be furious with her.

"Skye! Are you woolgathering again?"

She turned back guiltily to her friend. "Afraid so," she admitted. "What did you say?"

"I said, I think you should go ahead and go out with Mr. Denton."

"But he'll only be here another month or two. What'll I do when he's gone?" She paused. "Besides, I don't know if he even wants to see me anymore."

"I'll bet he does," Lyn said with confidence. "And as far as him leaving—maybe he'll take you with him."

Skye stared at her friend, shocked. "I could never leave the mountain."

"Why not?"

"You know why. I hate the city. And people here need me."

"That's for sure," Lyn said thoughtfully. "Well, maybe he'll stay here and run the recreation area."

Skye laughed shortly. "Fat chance. He thinks we're all weird. He's itching to get out of here."

Lyn shrugged. "Well, if you love each other, you'll work something out."

"Who said anything about love? He wants my body, that's all. There's nothing long-term about it, either. He just wants a woman to keep him happy while he has to be out here in the boonies."

The blond woman raised her eyebrows. "You sound bitter."

"I'm not," Skye denied quickly. "I'm just trying to explain why it would be stupid for me to get involved with him."

"You're being too logical about it. Just take it one day at a time."

Skye determinedly turned the conversation in a different direction. "Have you seen Tom around lately?" she asked. She'd already told Lyn about their emotional evening together.

"Sure have. He's one of the ones who's been giving Bob a hard time about taking a job with Denton Rec. He looks at it as a betrayal of Bob's loyalty to the settlement." She paused, a frown creasing her forehead. "In fact, I'm a little worried about the whole thing. I think some of the men are mad enough to do more damage than spray-paint this time."

"You don't think Tom's involved in that, do you?"

"Not directly, maybe. But he's bitter and everyone knows it. The younger guys look up to him, and they could do something crazy thinking they were doing it for Tom."

Skye nodded.

"Anyway," Lyn continued, "I worry about Bob working with that machinery down there. I wouldn't put it past them to tamper with it, and that could be dangerous."

"No kidding." Skye sat silently a moment and then took her leave, full of thought.

The next morning found her in the village early, a new packet of sketches in her bag. She'd run down the mountain as usual, just for the joy of it, although there had been no chase by Tom or any of the other settlement men. She felt a pang of regret even though she was basically glad that the game was passing out of phase. Times changed, whether you wanted them to or not.

As she emerged from the souvenir shop, she fingered the bills in her purse with delight. She'd never made so much money from her sketches before.

"You look happy this morning."

She jerked around and looked in the direction of the familiar voice. "Hi, Cole," she said, hesitating only briefly before she walked over to the bench where he sat. She felt a little shy. Partly because of the tension in which they'd parted before, and partly because she'd been thinking about Lyn's advice to go ahead and go out with Cole.

"Why the smile?" he asked.

She held out the roll of bills. "Look! I'm making great money on my sketches!"

"What type of sketches?"

She shrugged. "Just nature scenes, mostly charcoal. The tourists like them."

"Then the more tourists, the more successful you are," he said, a hint of baiting in his voice.

But she was too pleased to be drawn into an argument with him. "That's right. Maybe I'll get rich off of Denton Rec after all."

They smiled at each other for a moment longer than was appropriate, then they both looked away.

Cole was still smiling. "So...do you have plans for tonight?"

She shook her head.

"How would you like to go out for dinner?"

"To Dot's?" Dot's was the only restaurant in Crooked Fork.

"Umm, maybe not. How about driving into Colorado Springs for a fancy meal? Say, at the Broadmoor?"

She hesitated. The offer was tempting; she rarely left the settlement now, and it would be exciting to visit a city for one night, no matter how much she disliked them as a rule. And it would be even more exciting, she admitted to herself, to spend a special evening with Cole Denton. Despite the time they'd spent together, she didn't know him as well as she'd like to. On the other hand, she wasn't sure yet whether she wanted to get more deeply involved with him.

"Come on, please?" His voice was a perfect imitation of a small child's plea for candy, and the humor decided her.

"Okay. I'll go."

"I'll pick you up at six."

When she saw the look in Cole's eyes as she opened the door, she was glad she'd decided to dress up. She'd pressed the rose silk dress that was her only elegant item of clothing, and she'd washed and curled her hair. She regretted that she had no jewelry to complete the outfit, but his eyes told her she looked good to him.

They chatted easily during the long drive. At her prompting, Cole told her about his role in Denton Recreation. She learned that he'd taken over upon the death of his father, and that he'd found out that the organization had financial problems almost immediately.

"My brother John and I decided that we needed to specialize, and resort construction is what we came up with. John thinks the Crooked Fork project might be the final push Denton needs." He maneuvered a sharp curve in the road. "It's our biggest resort contract yet, and if it turns out to please our clients, we'll send our reputation skyrocketing."

"But you're worried?"

He nodded. "The opposition is slowing us down, putting us behind schedule."

"Some of the settlement people are changing their minds about Denton," she said. She told him about her conversation with Lyn.

"Bob seems like a good worker," he said. "I owe you for the idea of getting some local workers on the project right away. We've hired six men so far, and they're doing good work. But I'm still bothered by the sabotage."

"Have you had some problems?"

"Some. Nothing major, but there have been too many equipment foul-ups. I think someone may be sneaking in at night and messing with the machinery."

Skye frowned, thinking of what Lyn had said about the group of younger men who looked up to Tom. They might be behind it, but she didn't want to unjustly accuse anyone, so she didn't mention the possibility to Cole.

"Look. We're almost there."

As they topped a gentle rise in the landscape, the lights of Colorado Springs came into view. In the deepening dusk, with dark silhouettes of mountains as a backdrop, the town looked like a fairyland.

"It's beautiful," she said after a moment.

"Cities have their good moments," he said. Then he laughed. "Especially at night, when you can't see any dirt or air pollution."

They walked into the grand old hotel a few minutes later, and Skye drank in the sights. Ornate chandeliers sparkled overhead, and exotic ornaments filled lighted display cases. Her feet sank into the thick carpet.

Cole took her arm and led her across the opulent room. In minutes they were seated at a linen-covered table, with a view of the hotel's miniature lake and the emerging stars.

"I feel like a real country mouse," she admitted as she smiled at him across the table. "This is elegant."

"You fit in here just as well as you do in the mountains," he said. "You're not afraid to enjoy your own reactions to things, and you're not self-conscious."

She blushed, feeling warm inside, and looked down at her menu. The duck she ordered at Cole's recommendation was delicious, and they fell into a companionable silence as they ate their meals.

"Wow. That was rich," Skye said finally as she leaned back from the table. "But delicious."

"You did a pretty good job on it, I see," he teased as he looked at her nearly clean plate.

"I do love to eat," she said, laughing. "It's a good thing I get a lot of exercise running up and down that mountain. Otherwise, I'd be a blimp."

"That'll be the day."

As the waiter cleared their dishes away, the soft sounds of a dance combo filtered in from another room. Craning her neck to look for the music, Skye saw several couples dancing.

"That looks fun!" she exclaimed, then felt a flush creeping up her face. She should probably wait for him to ask her to dance.

"Let's give it a try."

As she stood, the thought of being in his arms made her shiver. "I've only been dancing a couple of times," she warned him to cover her nervousness. "I'm not very good at it."

"Neither am I, so we can be bad dancers together."

As they reached the dance floor, Skye paused by the window just as the full moon came out from behind a heavy cloud.

"Oh, no," she said. "I hope that full moon doesn't mean Lyn's going into labor tonight."

"Why should it?" he asked.

"It's just more likely that it will happen now than at any other time," she said, surprised that he didn't know what every child on the mountain did. "A full moon tends to bring on labor."

"More country folklore?"

"You don't believe it? Check the statistics sometime."

He pulled her into his arms. "Come on, let's dance. I didn't mean to make fun."

Her momentary irritation faded as she reveled in the soft music, the moonlight, and the feel of his arms around her.

She could tell quickly that Cole was far more experienced at dancing than he'd led her to believe. He moved effortlessly in time to the soft music, and under his gentle guidance she found herself feeling graceful and skilled, as well.

"Nice music, huh?"

She cocked her head, considering the quiet jazz. "Well, I don't know. It's a little too slow for me..."

"You make me feel my age, young lady," he said. "What kind of music do you like? Synthesizers? Heavy metal?"

"The truth is, I do like jazz," she said, laughing up at him. "We don't hear much of the latest rock on the mountain."

He chuckled and pulled her closer to him. For long moments they swayed together, and as the sensation of being enveloped in his strong arms overwhelmed her, the rest of the world faded away.

"You feel good in my arms," Cole whispered softly against her ear. His hands pulled her tighter against him, then stroked her hair.

As she listened to his whispered endearments and felt the comfort of his embrace, she sighed. When he held her, she had no desire for anything else in the world. It was a feeling of completion the likes of which she'd never known before, and the intensity of it was almost scary.

When the song ended he let go of her reluctantly, but kept a tight grasp on her hand. "It's hard for me to let you escape from my arms, once you're there," he said in a soft voice.

She looked up at him, wondering at the emotion she saw in his deep gray eyes. Her own feelings were getting dangerously intense, and she quickly let her gaze drop.

"Still afraid of me, Skye?"

She didn't answer. What could she say? She was more afraid of herself than of him. If it had only been a question of his emotions, she could have handled them. But she feared that her own deepening desires could lead her into behavior she'd regret later.

She looked up to find him regarding her closely, an unreadable expression in his eyes. "Do you want to dance again now, or would you rather walk around and look at the hotel shops before they close?"

"The shops, I think," she said. That would give her a chance to get a grip on her feelings outside of the heady realm of his arms.

He laughed. "Somehow, that's what I thought you would say." He led her off the dance floor and into the more brightly lit lobby.

Even though it was late, most of the hotel shops were brightly lit, and a surprisingly large number of people roamed up and down, window-shopping. Cole smiled as she studied everything on display in a ceramic shop's window.

"Look at this, Cole! It's just like Kronos!"

He bent down to inspect the statuette of a crow about to descend. "Who's Kronos?" he asked.

"I keep forgetting that you don't know that kind of thing," she said. She explained about the bird she and Gran had found. "Oh, and look. There's a man at the settlement who makes things like this." She indicated a set of tiny wooden animals.

"We can go inside, you know."

At the sound of stifled laughter in his voice, she looked up quickly. "What's so funny?"

"I've never seen you in an urban setting. I always thought of you as a nature-type person. But I see that you can get bit by the shopping bug, just like most Americans."

"You're right," she said, laughing. "I don't get to shop very often, but I make up in enthusiasm for what I lack in experience." She tugged at his arm. "Come on, come on! Let's go in and look around."

After what seemed like only a few minutes, the shopping area's lights started to flicker.

"Oh, no," she said. "Are they closing already?"

"It's eleven o'clock." She could tell that he was laughing at her again.

"You're kidding! We've been shopping for over an hour?"

He nodded. "Let's have one more dance before we head back to the rural life."

As they walked toward the dance floor again, hand in hand, she looked at him curiously. "You really don't like being out in the country, do you?"

"It's not as bad as I expected."

"But it's not good?"

He turned toward her at the dance floor's edge and pulled her into his arms as the music started. "I feel awfully isolated out there. It's far from the action of the world." He pulled her closer and they started to sway with the music. "That is, I feel isolated except when I'm with you."

The knowledge that she could help to assuage his loneliness made her feel curiously happy. "The city's not so bad when you're around, either," she said.

As they danced, Cole led them to a darkened corner of the floor, away from most of the other couples. She looked up at him quizzically.

"What..."

"Don't talk." In a moment his lips were on hers, making her swallow the question. Tender at first, he soon became more masterful, and Skye forgot to dance except for a marginally rhythmic motion as a concession to where they were.

"Ah, Skye. This is what I've been longing to do to you all evening." His arms tightened around her as his lips passed over the downy hairs at her temples. "This, and so much more."

His implication made her blush, but her mild protest was engulfed in his kiss as he took her lips again. The dance floor seemed to swirl around her, and she clung harder to him. He seemed the only steady force in her world.

As his kiss deepened, she felt a sharp yearning shoot through her body, and she twisted uncomfortably in his arms. Her cheeks were hot, she was breathing hard, and her head was spinning, but she didn't know whether to try to stop him or to beg him to go on.

He seemed to sense her confusion. With the faintest of sighs he released her lips and pulled her back onto the dance floor. "Okay, honey. Let's dance." As they swayed with the music again, she rested her head against his broad shoulder, enjoying the sensation of having someone else take charge.

As the song ended he brushed his lips lightly over the top of her head. She shivered. Even his slightest touch made her go weak inside.

"It's time to be heading back, I'm afraid," he said.

Reluctantly they walked back through the lush lobby. This time Skye's eyes were focused more on the man next to her than on the opulence of the hotel. The slight hint of gray at his temples made him look even more attractive than he would have otherwise, she decided. And with the hard lines of his face softened by the evening's relaxation, he looked at ease and devastating.

"I feel like I'm under a microscope."

"Sorry," she said, feeling a flush creep into her cheeks.

"It's okay. I just wish I knew what you were thinking when you looked at me like that."

She grinned at him. "That's my secret."

Cole drove the mountain roads a little more slowly now that night had fallen. Although the full moon cast a silvery light over the landscape, the roads were still narrow and required extra caution. It was almost two hours before he pulled up in front of her cabin.

"I'd like to come in and talk, Skye, but it's awfully late."

She smiled up at him, relieved that she wouldn't have to make a decision about how far to let his kisses go. At the same time, though, she felt a pang of regret at the thought of seeing him drive away into the night.

"At least I'll walk you to the door." He was out of the car and around to her side in a flash.

On the doorstep she looked up at him. "Did you have a good time tonight?" she asked.

"I enjoyed it, yes. For the most part."

She was puzzled by his choice of words. "What was wrong, Cole?"

His responding grin was slightly strained. "What was wrong is that I find it incredibly frustrating to be around you. I keep having these lecherous desires to take you off to some island retreat where I could have you all to myself and do all sorts of immoral things to you."

"Cole!"

"I'm just being honest," he said, his voice growing serious. "You're a beautiful young woman. Both inside and out." He lowered his lips to her forehead and brushed it chastely.

Then he raised his head and dropped his hands from her shoulders. "And I'd better get out of here before my baser instincts take over."

From inside the screen door, she watched as he strode back to his car. The engine roared to life and he flicked the headlights on.

Suddenly she saw a small form dash across the headlights' yellow glare. "Cole, look out!" she cried, but he couldn't hear her as he put the car into gear. He started to pull forward, but then jolted to a halt as he saw the small child bathed in the headlights' glow. Cole jumped immediately out of the car.

"What the devil... Who are you looking for, little fellow?"

"Skye? Where's Skye?"

She came out on the porch. "Jason? Is that you?" She thought she recognized Lyn's older child, but it was hard to tell in the dusky moonlight.

"Yes, it's me," the child cried as he ran toward her and hurled himself into her arms. "I'm scared."

"Well, of course you're scared, up here in the middle of the woods at night. What's the matter?"

He sniffed loudly. "Mommy keeps saying she wants you there. And then she hurts inside and Daddy makes me leave so I won't see her crying. But I could still hear her!" He burst out in a wail.

Cole knelt down beside them and used his handkerchief to wipe the child's grimy face. "What do you think's the matter with her, Skye?" he asked.

"I'm afraid she went into labor." She turned back to the child. "Jason, did you hear your Daddy or Mommy say anything about going to the hospital?"

"Daddy wants to take her but Mommy won't go. She keeps asking for you."

Skye stood quickly and lifted the child to rest against her shoulder. "Cole, can you drive me down to the settlement?"

"Of course."

In minutes they were in front of Lyn's shabby white house. Cole took the now sleepy Jason from Skye's arms and sat down on the porch swing while Skye hurried through the unlocked front door.

"How is she, Bob?" she asked the pale-looking man as he emerged from the bedroom.

"Skye. Thank God you're here."

A glance through the bedroom door showed her that Lyn was between pains; she had her eyes closed and seemed to be resting. She turned back to Bob, waiting.

"I'm worried about her," he said.

"Why is she here? Why not at the hospital?"

Bob shook his head. "She doesn't want to go at all. She hid the fact that she was in labor until a couple of hours ago, and now I'm afraid it's too late."

"But this is so dangerous." Skye shook her head. "I just got home now, and I wouldn't have even known what was going on if Jason hadn't come up the path to my place."

"Jason came up alone?" Bob clapped a hand to his forehead. "I told him to get his grandma to fetch you. Is he all right?"

"He's fine. But, Bob, I think we should try to get Lyn to the hospital. I have a bad feeling about trying to deliver this one myself."

"But you've done it before."

"I know. But something's worrying me this time." She paused, frowning. "Let me take a look at her, and then we'll see."

She walked into the bedroom just as Lyn's eyes opened. "Skye. I knew you'd come," the blond woman said weakly. Then her face contorted as another pain gripped her.

Skye held Lyn's hand, whispering encouragement until the pain passed. "How far apart are they?"

"Ten minutes. But they're different from before. I've been having two together..." She trailed off as another pain took her only a moment after the previous one had ended.

Skye gripped her hand until the pain ended. "Just rest a few minutes now. I'm going to talk to Bob."

Lyn nodded weakly and shut her eyes. Skye studied her a moment, and noticed how pale her skin was. She looked terribly weak and vulnerable, and she had a long ordeal ahead of her.

The sound of low male voices led her to the front porch, where Bob and Cole stood talking. Jason lay sleeping on the porch swing. When they heard her come out the door, both men spun to face her.

"I think we should take her to High Mesa," she told them. "She's having double-peaked contractions, and I don't like her coloring."

"Oh, no," Bob said, his face blanching whiter than Lyn's had been. "Is she going to be okay? Is she in trouble? Oh, God, if I lose her..."

"You're not going to lose her," Skye said briskly. "But we'd best get busy and hustle her to the hospital."

"Is there time?" Cole asked.

She nodded. "There's time, although it would have been better to take her earlier. She's going to be uncomfortable."

Skye went to convince Lyn that the hospital was the best place for her, while Bob and Cole drove the other two children over to Lyn's mother's house. By the time the two men had returned, Skye had talked Lyn into going to the hospital, and Cole insisted on driving since his was the bigger car.

After the doctor examined Lyn, he emerged from the room and headed straight for Skye. "You're the midwife up at Crooked Fork, aren't you?"

She nodded. "How is she, doctor?"

"It's best that you brought her in. I have a feeling we're in for a long haul here, and I'd like to give her something for the pain."

Once Lyn was drifting in a hazy half consciousness, the doctor took Skye and Bob out into the hall. "I've a suspicion the baby is breech," he said. "We'll hold off for a while, but we may need to do a cesarean."

Skye shivered, thinking of what could have happened had she tried to deliver the baby herself.

From then on it was just waiting. Cole took Bob off somewhere for coffee while Skye sat with Lyn, talking quietly, and when the two men came back she noticed that Bob looked more relaxed. Then Skye took a break and sank down into a waiting room chair beside Cole while Bob sat with his wife.

"You were smart to bring Lyn in," Cole said. "How'd you know to do it?"

She shrugged. "Just a feeling."

"What do you mean, exactly?"

"Well, her coloring has been bad all along, and she's had nausea. A difficult pregnancy sometimes means a difficult birth. And then the double contractions made me worry. They're so exhausting."

"So then your 'feeling' was based on the things you'd observed. Physical things, about Lyn."

"I guess so."

He frowned thoughtfully. "But you did deliver Lyn's other babies?"

She nodded. "Jason was born when Gran was still alive, so we did it together," she explained. "Then when Sarah was born, I delivered her alone."

"It's amazing to me that a twenty-two-year-old woman would have that sort of experience under her belt."

"Everyone's always expected it of me, so I did it."

"Do you like it?"

She rubbed the back of her neck with one hand, thoughtful. "Delivering babies is wonderful when all goes well," she said. "It's a beautiful thing to see the new parents' joy and hold this new life in your hands. But there are times when something goes wrong, and that's a terrible feeling. I always wonder if there's something else

I could have done to make it easier, if only I'd known more."

"Did you ever think about being a doctor? Or a nurse?"

She nodded. "When I went to college, that was my plan. To be a nurse practitioner. That way, I'd be better trained to do a lot of the stuff I do now but the time required for the education wouldn't be as long as to be a doctor."

"You should think about going back," he said. "You seem to have the knack for healing people, and if you'd combine that with more education..."

"But where the time or money would come from, I don't know," she said. "I think—"

Her comment was cut off by Bob. "They're going to have to do the cesarean," he said as he walked toward them. "But I wish you'd look in on her once more before they do it."

Skye hurried in immediately and sat down by her friend. "How are you feeling, hon?" she asked.

Lyn grimaced. "Terrible," she said. "I'm still having the same kind of contractions as before, and they're not getting any closer together."

Skye rested her hands on Lyn's swollen stomach. She could feel the surging life there. "Don't worry, baby," she said softly. "We'll get you out somehow."

Lyn chuckled, then winced as another pain took her. "I'm glad you're here," she murmured when it was over.

Then the doctor bustled in and Lyn was carried off to another room. Skye rejoined Cole and Bob, a sigh escaping her.

"You're feeling left out, aren't you?" Cole asked.

"A little. I'm glad she's here, but I'll miss seeing the baby born."

After what seemed like hours, the doctor emerged and beckoned to Bob. Moments later, he emerged again from his wife's room, his face bright with joy. "I have another little boy," he said. "And a healthy, sleeping wife."

"You're a very lucky man," Cole said. Skye added her congratulations, wondering at the wistful tone of Cole's voice.

"You two should go on home," Bob said. "I'll be here all day." Then he paused and looked at Cole. "That is, if I can have the day off?"

Cole grinned. "Of course," he said. Then he and Skye left, waving off Bob's thanks.

In the gravel driveway outside her cabin, Cole pressed a small package into her hand. "Here. I forgot to give you this before."

She fumbled with the paper and uncovered the tiny statuette of a crow that she'd admired earlier in the ceramic shop. "Cole, you shouldn't have!" she cried, turning the statue in her hands. "It's even more lifelike than I realized. But when did you get in without my seeing you?"

Cole laughed. "There was plenty of opportunity. You were so engrossed in your shopping that there was no problem at all." He reached across the front seat to her and gently touched her face. "Get some rest, Skye. You've had a long night."

"So have you," she said. "That was good of you to bring us down to the hospital."

"They're a nice family." He got out of the car and opened her door for her. "Now go sleep."

But sleep didn't come quickly for Skye. A scared, excited feeling that was new to her kept her tossing restlessly, and she couldn't shake Cole's image from her mind.

Don't count on him, an inner voice nagged. She could sense that he was holding a part of himself back from her; he never spoke of his feelings or the future. Whether it was city sophistication or some past hurt, he obviously wasn't interested in anything long-term with her.

And yet... when she thought of the way he looked at her, the excited feeling came back. She couldn't help but feel that something more would happen between them before it was all over.

Not if I don't get any rest, she told herself, bunching up her pillow. But it was several hours before she slept.

Chapter Six

She was running, running down the mountain for the sheer joy of it, dodging trees and cactus plants, her eyes alert for snakes or other dangers. Her sketches were safely in her bag, and she felt the exuberance of the chase even though there was no one running after her.

She wondered if Cole could really catch her, as he'd boasted once. She hadn't seen him for several days, since the night Lyn's baby was born, but he'd loomed large in her thoughts. She had put the crow statuette on her dining table, and every meal found her thinking of the man who'd bought it for her.

He had been so kind that night. He hadn't had to take the time to help Lyn and Bob; he could easily have left them to fend for themselves. Her opinion of him had risen as she'd seen his cool head and caring heart during the tense situation. He wasn't really the heartless executive she'd first thought him to be.

Lost in thought, she raced on, hardly paying attention to the environment around her. Dodging the small animals' holes and spiny plants that grew so readily on the dry hillside was almost automatic after so many years of doing it, and the knowledge that Tom Zale wasn't chasing her anymore lulled her into a sense of security.

"What's your rush, lady?"

The hard voice brought her to an abrupt halt, and one look at the leering face before her made her realize she'd been too careless. She sidestepped from the man's path and shot her eyes around, gauging her escape route. She had no doubt that she could outdistance this pudgy fellow; it was just a question of choosing her moment.

"Just cool down," he said. "You're not going anywhere." Then he turned halfway around. "Come on, boys, we've got her at last."

Two more men materialized out of the bushes, and Skye's eyes widened with fear. One of them held a length of rope, and the other had a bulge in his jacket pocket that looked suspiciously like a gun.

"What . . . what do you want?"

"Well, now, that depends," the first man drawled. "For starters, you can give us your bag."

She hesitated. There was very little money there, but her sketches were important enough to fight for. "I don't have any money. . ."

"We'll see about that!" The man approached her and grabbed for the bag. Frightened by the harsh note in his voice, Skye let him have it without a struggle.

He pawed through it rapidly while the other two men watched her. "This ain't worth nothing," he said in disgust as he extracted the five dollar bill from her wallet. Then he pulled out the packet of sketches.

"Don't..." Skye cried as he opened the paper she'd wrapped them in and carelessly thumbed through. Several of the sketches flew away in the wind and Skye watched them, swallowing hard. All that work gone.

Finally the man threw down the rest of the sketches in disgust. "Aw, just some old pictures," he said.

"Now that you've messed up my things, would you please step aside? I've got work to do." She managed to make the words sound confident, although she was quaking inside.

"Well, now, just wait a minute," the man said. "We've seen you running down the mountain before, with your boyfriend chasing you. But the last couple of times, we noticed that he wasn't here anymore. We figured you must be kind of lonely."

She stalled for time, eyeing the three men. "Who are you? I've never seen you before."

"We're staying at the new cottages down by the village. Doing some fishing in these parts. But a man can only fish so many times, and then he gets a hankering for some other sport." The two other men laughed and nodded, approaching a few steps closer to Skye.

She edged away from them. "What are your names?"

"Tom, Dick, and Harry," said the one with the gun-like bulge, and all three of them laughed.

With a shiver, she read the intentions in their eyes. They were looking at her as if she were some new toy, and she shuddered as she realized what game they wanted to play.

"Well, I've got some things to do down in the village, so if you don't mind, I'll be running along now," she said, marveling at the quiet, reasonable sound of her voice.

"Oh, but we do mind, pretty lady. We're not finished with you yet. That should be pretty easy to figure out, even for a mountain hick like you."

Her face grew hot at the insult, but her anger changed to fear as two of the men came steadily closer. Frantically she looked from one side to the other. There was a row of trees that lined the creek on her left; on the right was an impassable-looking mass of prickly berry bushes. She knew immediately that the creek side would be her best escape route; she was more familiar with the lay of the land there, and even her skill at dodging natural barriers couldn't shield her from the rough prickles of those berry bushes.

She assessed her three opponents quickly. The ringleader looked chunky, but the muscular bulges under his shirt suggested strength, too. If she could stay out of his reach, he probably couldn't catch her; he looked more strong than fast.

The two men approaching her were a different story. They looked younger, and the one with the rope looked a little scared. He wasn't as muscular as the ringleader, but he was leaner. He was probably the fast one. The one with the gunlike bulge looked wiry, and he carried his few pounds of extra weight well. He had an evil gleam in his eyes, and she realized immediately that he was the most dangerous of the three.

As the two men walked slowly toward her, she stepped backward. She felt adrenaline surge through her, every muscle was tight and prepared, and every nerve alert. She crouched down slightly as she took another step backward.

"Don't run away, pretty girl. We'll treat you real good." The man with the bulge had a nasty undertone to his voice that validated her first impression of him. They were within two yards of her now.

"Grab her!"

At the shouted command from the ringleader, the two men closed in. She feinted to the right, then ran a few steps back up the mountain. When the man with the rope dived at her, she sidestepped and hurtled herself full speed down the pathway.

She was free! She'd—

The hand locked around her wrist before she had time to finish the thought. It was the ringleader. He'd moved more quickly than she'd expected. His grip jerked her to a halt and, losing her balance, she plunged to the ground.

His leering face was right over her. "Nice try, baby. I like a girl who fights. Makes things more interesting."

"Please," she said, her breath coming in short gasps. "Please, let me go."

He laughed unpleasantly, then looked up at his scrambling companions. "She's lost her spirit now," he said. "This is going to be easy."

The words were scarcely out of his mouth when Skye jerked her hand free from his grip. With her feet she pushed off from him, hard, causing him to lose his balance. He stumbled sideways, and Skye struggled to her feet. Gulping for air, she took one desperate leap away. Then another. Then—

"Got her!"

The wiry one with the nasty voice had her by the ankle, and again she crashed to the ground as he jerked at her. Dimly she noticed the pain in her knees and palms as her body encountered the rough grit of the hillside. The impact made her head swim.

The wiry one's hand climbed up the length of her leg, well under her skirt, and she cringed in horror.

He laughed when he saw her reaction to him. "Hey, boys. I think she likes me."

The ringleader had risen from the ground where her sharp kick had made him fall, and he lumbered over. "Feisty little wench, ain't she?" He reached out and grabbed the front of her shirt, pawing for the buttons.

She forced her body to relax for a moment, her heart sinking as she felt her shirt rip. The ringleader spread the torn edges apart and let out a whistle.

"Hey, Joe-Bob. Looky here."

The wiry one mercifully stopped his explorations of her legs as he raised his head to look at her. Her hands were free now, although the man named Joe-Bob lay heavily across her legs.

The ringleader's hands reached toward her breasts. She dug her stinging palms into the sandy grit and came up with two handfuls of it. Just before his palms made contact with her, she flung the grit into their sniggering faces.

"What the—"

The wiry one rolled off, clawing at his eyes. She scrambled to her feet and tore down the path, putting as much distance as she could manage between herself and them. Her breath was coming in choked gasps now, but she forced herself to keep going.

Behind her, she heard racing footsteps. The third one! The one with the rope! He was gaining on her, and in her weakened state she knew she couldn't outpace him. But she remembered the fear she'd glimpsed in his eyes.

As he came up behind her she whirled fiercely, sticking out her palms to block him. Startled he came to an abrupt halt, only narrowly maintaining his balance.

"You'd better not touch me. I'm a witch." She fixed him with a tight, cold glare that she'd used to scare misbehaving settlement children. "I can put spells on people to make them sick."

Her harsh words caused him to take an involuntary step backward, and his hands, which had been reaching out for her, dropped to his sides.

"Aw, you're lying," he said uncertainly.

"I put a blindness curse on your friends," she said gesturing back to where the other two men were. He looked back fearfully. They both still crouched where she'd left them, rubbing at the dirt and grit in their eyes.

"Holy Mary." The young man took another backward step away from her.

"I'll do it to you, too, if you try to follow me. Or if you look at me that way again," she added, noticing that his eyes had strayed to her exposed breasts.

Immediately his eyes came back to her face.

"I mean it," she warned, then turned and ran at full speed down toward the village.

No footsteps followed her, but she didn't slow down. Hot tears started to stream down her cheeks. Now she had time to be scared.

She had to get to the village. She couldn't risk going home and having them find out where she lived. Finally, gasping, her lungs almost bursting, she reached the edge of the village. She clutched the edges of her torn shirt together and stopped trying to hold back the tears. Walking blindly, she headed toward the general store.

"Hey, little lady. What happened to you?"

It was old Pop Jones's voice, coming from somewhere in the direction of the store. A moment later he was beside her, his old arms surprisingly strong as he helped her into a chair on the store's porch.

Cole walked up the street toward the Sunshine General Store at a quick pace. It was a beautiful morning, and the work at the site was progressing well. Local opposition seemed to be dying out, thanks partly, he thought, to his relationship with Skye and to her friends Lyn and Bob.

He still felt wary about Skye. She was too young to know her own feelings, and though her response to his kisses was sweetly passionate, he didn't trust that that response would last. Deidre, too, had felt passion for him at first, but that passion had quickly faded when she'd started looking around at other men.

But despite his wariness, he couldn't stop thinking about Skye any more than he could keep his hands off of her. And this morning, he couldn't bring himself to feel bad about her.

Suddenly he realized that the woman in question was right there on the store's porch, and he felt a pleasant, excited sensation as he slowed to a halt in front of her.

"Just lazing around this morning, are you?" he asked in a teasing voice.

She didn't answer; in fact, she hardly seemed to see him.

He looked at her more closely. She was filthy! Her legs and arms were covered with brown dust, and her blouse which she was holding together as she cowered in the chair, was ripped and mangled.

He felt a pounding rage start to burn in him. Sinking down beside her, he took her free hand. "What happened to you? Who did this?"

For the first time she seemed to focus on him. "Some of your damned tourists," she said.

He wasn't sure what she was talking about, but he could see that she was hurting. Lord, what had they done to her? He reached up to put an arm around her slumped shoulders.

"Don't touch me," she said, jerking away.

Pop Jones emerged from the dark interior of the store. He was shaking his head and making clucking sounds with his tongue. "Here, little lady. You just wrap this around you," he said, slipping a large old shirt around her shoulders. "And I brought you a root beer to drink."

When he saw the way she accepted the old man's help, Cole felt a surge of ridiculous jealousy. Fiercely he fought it down. "Skye, tell us who did this to you."

She looked at him with resentment in her eyes. "How should I know their names? They were some of the new folks this town is crawling with."

"Don't you remember anything about them, honey?" asked Pops. "Tell us about what happened so we can let the sheriff know."

"One of them was named Joe-Bob," she said. "They said they were staying in one of the new cabins. They were on a fishing trip, I think."

"How many were there?" Cole asked, his heart sinking.

"Three."

"Oh, Lord," he said. "Did they... I mean, should we get you to a doctor?"

"I'm all right. I got away from them in time."

"How'd you do it, honey?" asked Pops.

As she explained how she'd thrown sand in their eyes and dodged away from them, Cole's eyes widened in admiration. It took a clear head to outfox opponents who were bigger than you and outnumbered you, as well.

She seemed to be coming out of shock as she spoke, and when she finished her explanation, Cole asked, "Are you feeling better?"

She gave him a cold stare. "What concern is it of yours?" she asked.

Why was she so furious at him? Surely she didn't blame him... But of course, she had every right to be upset and irrational after what she'd been through. "Is there anything I can do to help you?" he asked gently.

"Stop trying to be so helpful! You can't make it better!"

"I know I can't take back what they did to you, Skye—"

"It's your fault! Don't you realize that it's completely your fault that this happened to me?"

Cole was bewildered and starting to feel defensive. "My fault? Why are the actions of three idiots my fault?"

"You'd see it if you could open your eyes to anyone but yourself." Her eyes were flashing furiously at him now, and she'd risen from her seat. Even with her torn clothes and dirt-covered body, she had a dignity that surrounded her like an aura.

"What do you mean? Tell me, honey."

"I'm not your honey!"

He was beginning to get impatient. "What are you talking about?"

"You really don't see it, do you? You don't see that this never would have happened without Denton Recreation building cabins for outsiders to stay in." She shook her head in disgust and sank down on the bench again.

So that was it. She was blaming him because of the changes Denton had caused on the mountain. "Things always change," he said gently. "If Denton hadn't come in, someone else would have. Your quiet way of life was bound to end."

"The hell it was!"

"No, Skye, he's right." Cole turned in surprise to the old man. He'd forgotten Pops was there. "I don't like the changes any better than you do," Pops said. "But they had to happen. It's been coming on for more years than you realize."

"Aw, Pops. That's not true." Tom Zale and several of his cronies had materialized at the bottom of the store's porch steps.

"I'm going to get the sheriff," Cole said, and turned toward the village's main street. Behind him, he heard Zale's voice rising as he seemed to realize that Skye was hurt.

"What happened to her?" Zale was asking. "Who did it?"

"What did they look like? We'll get them," he heard Zale's friends chip in. Cole walked faster. It was easy to visualize the vigilante action that would start up when the settlement people realized that one of their own had been hurt.

Damn! Cole felt the blood pounding hard in his head as he strode rapidly toward the sheriff's office. He genuinely believed that Denton Recreation would be good for Crooked Fork; the area was incredibly poor, and he knew that young people had been leaving it in increasing numbers for the past few years. He'd also heard that several mining companies had been considering the area for new operations before Denton had bought up the prime land. And that would have changed the place's character far more dramatically than Denton's recreational facility would.

Still he felt a twinge of guilt as he remembered Skye's tear-streaked face. His hands clenched into hard fists at the thought of the three men who had attacked her. He'd like to see them shot.

As the twilight settled around her cabin that night, Skye felt a tiny shiver of fear break through the numbness she'd drawn around herself in self-protection.

She'd finally gotten Tom and his friends to leave after listening to a proud explanation of their exploits. They'd run the three men out of town in the end, but not before they'd given them some injuries. Serious ones, she suspected, although they'd been vague about exactly what they had done. Tom had wanted to spend the night there, but she'd finally convinced him that she would be all right alone.

Now she wasn't so sure about the decision. What if the three men came back? She shuddered as the memory of those rough hands on her body gripped her. She'd taken a long bath and she was physically clean, but the memories wouldn't come off with soap and water.

A sound outside the door made her jump up. She was halfway across the room, the fireside poker in her hand, before she identified the sound. It was only Farimer, scratching at the door in the hopes of getting the leftovers of her dinner.

Farimer would protect her, she thought gratefully. Just as he always did. The huge mongrel would bark fiercely at the three men if they came, and he wouldn't hesitate to use his teeth, either.

But what about the wiry man's gun? Had it really been a gun? He hadn't shot at her; but then, he hadn't really had a chance. By the time he'd gotten the sand out of his eyes, she'd been long gone. What if he came back tonight, looking for revenge, and shot Farimer?

Hurriedly she went out onto the steps with her almost untouched dinner plate. "Here, boy," she said to the large black beast. While he wolfed down the food, she patted his shaggy back. "You'll take care of me, won't you?"

The sound of crackling branches and footsteps made her jerk up, then shrink against the door. Why wasn't

Farimer barking? As she peered fearfully into the darkening forest, a familiar figure emerged.

It was Cole! She sighed with relief. Farimer looked up at him without much interest, then went back to licking the plate of food shiny clean.

"What are you doing here?" she asked, annoyed at how shaky her voice sounded.

"I thought you might like some company tonight. This place is pretty isolated."

"Still playing the concerned executive?"

He walked toward her. "I know you're upset with me. And I think I understand why. But that doesn't make this lonely place any safer for you tonight."

"I already turned down plenty of offers of company."

"But that was probably before it got dark, right?"

He was perceptive, she realized reluctantly. He knew how independent she was, but he also sensed her fear. And he was right that things had seemed a lot safer before the sun had gone down.

But he was the reason she had to worry. If it wasn't for Denton Recreation, those men would never have come to Crooked Fork.

"I don't want anyone around," she said. "I want to be alone."

He looked at her closely for a long moment. His gray eyes were unreadable, but their gaze was intense. "I don't think you mean that, Skye."

"I do mean it!"

"Then how come you're so jumpy?"

Ignoring his question, she bent down and picked up the plate Farimer had licked clean. "If I wasn't so mad at you, I'd thank you for coming up and checking on me.

But as you can see, I'm completely fine. So goodbye." She turned and opened the cabin door.

As she stepped up into the cabin, she felt his hand on her shoulder. "Listen to me for a minute," he said.

His touch aroused a sudden, unwelcome memory of the times he'd held her close to him. She stood stock-still, waiting.

"It's probably perfectly safe for you up here. But there is a chance that those men will come back. Your friend Tom gave them reason to be upset."

"What do you mean?"

"By the time the sheriff got up to their cabin, they were gone. He would have taken them into custody, but Tom Zale and his buddies had already run them out of town."

"I know. They told me."

"The neighbors who saw the fight said that Tom did some pretty nasty stuff to them. It's just possible that they'll come back looking for revenge."

"Farimer will take care of me," she said uncertainly.

"Farimer's not bullet-proof. And neither are you."

She started to shake involuntarily. She couldn't stop it. "Why did you come up here and scare me more?" she cried. "I was frightened enough already!"

"Skye, I—"

"I used to be able to live here alone! Now I don't know if I can anymore! Nothing's the same as it used to be. Nothing! And it's your fault." To her horror, the last words came out choked and she felt the hot tears start to press against her eyes. She turned away from him to hide the fact that she was crying.

Firm hands descended onto her shoulders and she felt herself being guided into the cabin. Her vision still blurred with tears, she moved helplessly where he guided her. He removed the forgotten plate from her hands and set it aside; then he pressed her into her rocking chair and knelt down in front of her.

"Skye, I'm terribly, terribly sorry about what happened today. There's no excuse for men who behave like that."

She couldn't reply; she could only sniffle. He took a handkerchief out of his pocket and offered it to her. She didn't want to take any help from him. But even less did she want her nose to drip in front of him. She took the handkerchief.

He waited while she wiped her eyes and nose. Then he spoke. "I can understand why you're blaming what happened on Denton Rec. And on me."

"But there's nothing you can do about it now."

"Not really." He put his hand on hers where it rested on the rocking chair's edge. "Crooked Fork has been discovered now, and there's no going back to the way it used to be. In my opinion, it would have been discovered by someone else if not by me. But I know you disagree."

She nodded, then paused, remembering Pop Jones's words. "Maybe it would have, Cole," she said reluctantly. "But it just seems like it's happening so fast."

"I know." He squeezed her hand. "And I want to help you get through what's happened to you. I know you weren't prepared for crime to come into your life."

She shuddered again, remembering the three men.

"I want to stay with you tonight." He held up a hand as she started to protest. "I know. You don't want me to stay. But I'm going to. Your only choice in the matter is whether I stay inside or out."

"Cole, I don't want you to..." She trailed off. How could she tell him that she didn't want to risk getting involved with him again? That if he stayed the night, she'd be tempted to go to him?

"If you want, I'll stay on your porch. I just want to make sure that you're safe. For my own peace of mind, as well as yours."

She gave up. "You can stay inside, I guess."

He looked up at her. "I'll try to behave myself in a respectable way, ma'am," he said.

She smiled reluctantly at the gentle joke. It was hard to stay angry with the man in front of her. Those gray eyes, which had seemed so cold when she'd first encountered them, could be unbelievably persuasive.

He squatted down by the pillows she had stacked on the braided rug. "I don't want to make you talk more about this morning," he said. "But are you really okay?"

"Yes," Skye said softly. "But all of my sketches are lost," she explained in a rising voice. "I was taking them down to sell at the souvenir shop, and those men took my bag and threw all my stuff around."

"That's too bad," he said. "Do you need anything? Do you need some money to get through the week?"

She shook her head. "No, I've got some savings. I just feel lucky that I got away from them in time."

"Don't underestimate yourself. It was quick thinking, not luck that saved you." There was admiration in his eyes. "You really kept your head. It's not many women—many men, either, for that matter—who could get away from three big guys."

"I was pretty scared," she admitted. "But I'm used to the mountain. All those times I got chased down it helped me out."

Cole nodded. "Maybe there's more value in that game than I realized," he said.

He settled down on the couch and she offered him a drink. As she made it for him, she felt something unknot inside of her. She hadn't realized before how tense she'd felt. Living alone was wonderful in some ways, but after this morning's traumatic experience, Cole's presence offered welcome security.

"Here you go." She handed him his drink and then sank down into the rocker to sip at her own glass of wine. Surreptitiously she studied him. He had rough, strong hands that looked oversized on her lightweight glassware, and he was dressed, as usual, in simple work clothes.

"Why do you dress like your workers?" The question slipped out before she had time to consider whether or not it was appropriate.

He looked down at his faded blue work shirt and jeans. "I get to be a mess working at the site. These are practical. And comfortable."

"Don't most managers wear suits?"

"Not good ones," he said. "The men need to be shown how to do things sometimes, or one of them may need a hand on a job. I'm available to do things in these clothes that I couldn't do if I was wearing a suit."

She nodded, then looked at him with more curiosity. He intrigued her, in spite of her intention to keep him at a distance. He was always fun to talk to, and he'd seen and done so many things. People who'd had broad experiences in life were few and far between on the mountain.

"Have you done much traveling?" she asked him.

"Some," he said. "I've been to South America on a research project. And I backpacked in Europe the year after college." He looked off into the distance, his eyes unfocused. "And I've seen Southeast Asia, but that wasn't by choice."

"Tell me about your favorite places."

"Are you sure you want to get me started on this?" he asked, grinning at her.

She nodded eagerly, and he launched into a colorful description of his hand-to-mouth existence while he'd backpacked Europe. She listened to the way he described the places he'd been with delight. He knew how to bring them to life, so that she could see the Swiss Alps, hear the noises of the busy Paris streets, and smell the rich Dutch chocolate.

She asked eager questions whenever he paused. Finally he held up his hand. "Whoa!" he said, laughing. "We've got plenty of time to continue this discussion another time. I feel like I've been doing a monologue these past two hours."

"Will we really have plenty of time?"

At the wistful sound of the question he looked at her sharply. "What do you mean?"

"I just want to hear as much as I can about the places you've been. I've never met anyone who's been abroad before. And I don't know how much longer you'll be around." As she said the words, Skye felt a sinking feeling deep inside. She shouldn't have said it aloud. That made his departure seem like a reality.

He looked at her with an expression she couldn't read. Was it hope? And why? But almost immediately the expression was gone and he patted the couch beside him. "Come sit here," he said.

She walked the short distance to the couch and sank down beside him, her eyes unable to leave his.

"It's true that the site is getting close to completion. At least, my stage of things will be done soon." He touched her face softly. "But we'll have some time to spend together yet. If you want to. I'll make sure of it."

It wasn't what she wanted to hear. Some time together wasn't much compared to the way the days and weeks would stretch out after he'd gone. But she had no right to expect to see him again, no claim on his time. She forced a cheerful smile on her face.

"All right, then. I'll let you stop for tonight." She paused wistfully. "But I do wish I could see those places you were talking about. They sound marvelous."

"I thought you never wanted to leave the mountain."

"I don't. Not permanently. But I'd like to see other places and then come home."

His arm slid around her shoulders, and again he touched her face. When she looked at him, there was a strange expression in his eyes. "How did I ever find a woman like you tucked away on this mountain?"

She felt the color creep into her cheeks. "What do you mean, like me?"

"You're such a curious mixture of tradition and excitement. I never know quite what to expect when I talk with you." Gently he brushed his lips across her forehead.

Her heart started to pound at the gentle touch, and a warmth spread through her body. Being here, next to him, was so bittersweet; she felt safe and comfortable, and yet unbearably agitated, as if something very new and very intense was about to happen.

Some of the confusion she felt must have shown in her eyes when she looked up at him.

"Have you any idea of what those eyes of yours do to me?" His voice was hoarse.

She shook her head, her eyes still locked with his. The tension in his voice was confusing yet exhilarating.

"Then I'll have to show you," he murmured. He lowered his lips to hers.

They had kissed before, but this was somehow different. This was tender, with an indefinable promise in the way he held her.

When she opened her lips, he tightened his arms around her, pulling her across his lap before he plunged his tongue into her waiting mouth. His hands tangled in her hair, then followed it down to the middle of her back in long strokes.

The feel of his caresses was drugging, almost intoxicating. His lips left hers and she felt his warm breath against her ear. He pushed back her hair and took her earlobe softly between his lips, then sucked lightly, and she gasped at the way the sensation coursed through her body.

"You're so responsive," he murmured. "So ready to feel with me." He nibbled lightly at her ear again, then trailed a long line of kisses down her neck. She threw her head back, delighting in the gentle seduction and the faint, musky scent of him.

Where will it end? a nagging voice in the back of her mind questioned. She silenced the voice defiantly. Being in his arms felt so good, so right. She didn't want to pull away from him. Never before had her body felt so alive; every nerve tingled and every muscle felt subtly tautened. His big body was wrapped around her like a blanket, and the sensation was so good that she shuddered.

Hesitantly, she ran her hands over his shoulders as his mouth continued to create spots of almost unbearable heat around her throat. Her hands grew bolder as she explored his bulky shoulders with curious hands.

"That's right. Touch me. Get to know me." His voice was husky, his breath hot on her neck.

Gently he shifted her on his lap so that her back was pressed against his chest. From behind, he rained kisses over the tiny hairs at her temple while his hands rose slowly from her waist to her breasts. Gently he cupped the warm fullness, and his quickened breathing matched hers.

She felt a flash of fear as she remembered the rough hands that had almost touched her there this morning. But it was gone almost as fast as it had come. This was nothing like that. This was tender and gentle, and it was something she wanted as much as he did.

Still, she wasn't prepared for the way his searching, gently scratching fingernails felt through the thin material of her blouse. As they brushed across both peaks in a light but insistent rhythm, she gasped at the shivers that coursed through her body. "Oh, Cole!" she whispered. Her head fell back against his shoulder and she felt the blood pumping hotly through her body, bringing a flush to her face and neck. Her breasts felt swollen as his hands continued to brush lightly across the hardening tips.

"Does this feel good to you?" he asked hoarsely against her ear.

"Yes, Cole," she whispered. She felt an overpowering urge to touch him, feel him, and she reached her hands back to stroke his sides. The action made her breasts surge forward to rest more heavily in his hands, and she heard his sharp intake of breath.

"Lord, Skye. Every move you make seduces me," he murmured as his hands stroked her. Then she felt him sliding the buttons of her blouse open.

"I should stop you. I shouldn't let you do this."

She didn't even know she'd spoken aloud until she heard him reply.

"Don't make me stop. I need this so badly." One of his hands slipped inside her shirt. Lazily it made concentric circles, starting at the outer fullness of her breast and moving in. When he finally reached the tip, he used his fingernail again to create an unbearably sensual, stroking rhythm.

She twisted against him, her breath coming in gasps. Behind her, she could hear his quickened breathing. His other hand was loosening the lower buttons of her blouse, and then she felt him pulling it loose from the waistband of her skirt.

"I want to see you, Skye," he whispered. "May I? Will you show yourself to me?"

The blunt question startled her, but a small frisson of excitement traveled up her spine at the thought of his eyes on her nakedness. Before her logical side could stop it, she whispered, "Yes, Cole. I want you to see me."

With gentle hands he turned her around, lifting her as though she weighed no more than a child. He perched her on his lap again, facing him. In the process, her shirt had fallen closed. He looked into her eyes for a long moment, and she could feel his excitement. Then, slowly, his eyes traveled downward as his hands parted the front of her shirt.

She watched his eyes, and was rewarded by the desire that flared there as he looked at her body. Then his eyes rose again to meet hers, and she could see from the corner of her eye the rapid rise and fall of his chest.

"You're the most beautiful woman I've ever seen."

She felt the heat rise to her cheeks. He made his desire for her so obvious. But there was something about the tender way he touched her that made her reluctant to call a halt to their lovemaking. He treated her so tenderly, almost as if he loved her. But she knew that he didn't, and couldn't....

His arms slid around her then, and he pressed his lips to hers, crushing her breasts against his broad chest. Then he strung a long garland of kisses down her neck and beyond, until his face rested between her breasts.

"I can feel your heart pounding," he whispered up to her as his hands cupped her breasts. Then his mouth pressed wetly over one rosy peak, and his tongue circled it in a round of increasing intensity.

Sensual flames shot through her body, creating a heat within her that was unlike anything she'd ever felt before. Unable to stop herself, she pushed against him, letting more of her breast surge forward into his hungry mouth while her fingers tangled in his hair. The caresses he made in response rendered her dizzy, and her head spun as she clung to him.

Just a minute more, she thought, and then she would stop this. The way her body felt was too strange and too frightening. And the way her skirt was creeping up her legs was too wanton. And the way Cole's hardness pressed against her left her in no doubt about his extreme arousal. Just a minute more...

As if he'd heard her thoughts, he eased himself away from her breast and met her lips again, stifling the protests that were rising to her lips. His tongue plunged into her warm wetness, more aggressively this time, creating an explosion of feeling as he searched her mouth. She was still dizzy, and her breath came hard as she felt the roughness of his shirt brushing back and forth against the tips of her breasts. She could smell the slight male scent of him rising from his heated body.

Finally he lifted his lips from hers. He drew a deep breath and met her eyes. "What do we do now, Skye?"

he asked softly, his hand brushing a strand of hair back from her face. From the corner of her eye she noticed that he was trembling ever so slightly.

"We have to stop now, I think," she whispered, her eyes locked into his.

"Are you sure we can?" His hands moved slightly so they cupped the fullness of her breasts while his thumbs teased the tips. He smiled as he heard her sharp intake of breath.

"See what I mean, Skye? We can't stop. I can feel how you want me. I feel how soft you are, how you respond when I touch you. I want to show you all the pleasure a man can give a woman." As he talked to her in a low, mesmerizing voice, his hands continued their maddening love play on her breasts until she was gasping. Still their eyes were locked together, and she knew that he sensed every nuance of her response to his touch.

"Please, Cole..."

"Please what? I don't know what you're asking of me." His voice had a rasping quality.

One of his hands slid down to the hem of her skirt and slowly skimmed up her leg. She tried to sway away from him, but he held her easily in place. His hand continued its journey until she felt it massaging the side of her hip, and a wave of panic washed over her at the invasion. "No, Cole! Stop it!" she cried, and pulled away from him more earnestly.

For a terrifying moment he held her in the same position, and his hands continued their sensual attack. Competing with her fear she felt a raging desire to let this man do as he pleased with her. The conflict made her go still, and he seemed to read it in her eyes.

"Ah, Skye. I want you so much." His hands slid slowly away from her body, and his fingers intertwined with hers. She could feel their slight trembling, and the way his chest rose and fell told her what effort it required of him to control his desire. Their eyes locked together for a long moment, and what she saw in him was too raw, too primitive for her to handle.

She scrambled off his lap and moved to the window, staring off into the darkness of the night, her head spinning with confusing thoughts. She had wanted him to make love to her. There was no way around it. He had aroused her to heights she'd never imagined, and yet her body knew that there was further to go.

She longed to make that journey with him as her guide. But she feared the pain and loss that would follow, inevitably, in giving herself to a man who couldn't be counted on to be there for her afterward.

Feeling him approaching behind her, she stiffened slightly, and he seemed to notice the slight motion. "It's all right, Skye. I think I have myself under control." His voice held the faintest trace of amusement.

"Are you laughing at me?" she asked. She'd felt so moved by the experience, but he seemed to be taking it lightly enough.

Large hands descended onto her shoulders and turned her gently around. "No, my sweet. I'm not laughing at you in the slightest way. If anything, I'm laughing at myself."

"Why?" she asked.

"I'm laughing at the way a thirty-five-year-old man can be brought to the level of an adolescent, shaking with his need for a beautiful woman but afraid to fulfill it." He shook his head ruefully and tilted up her chin with one finger. "I'm sorry, Skye. I'm sorry to frighten you. But my desire for you grows greater each time I'm near you, and someday. . . ."

"Someday what?"

"Nothing." He turned away from her and crossed his arms over his chest. "Sometimes I think I've been away from the city too long."

She felt hot tears rise and she shut her eyelids firmly, feeling the tears press against them. He talked as if his desire for her was a simple matter of physical need, a need that he could have satisfied easily in the city. "Well, you'll be going back soon, right?" she asked, forcing her voice to sound natural and easy.

He turned and met her eyes, his own dark and unreadable. For a moment he scrutinized her, and she forced herself to smile brightly at him. Then he sighed heavily. "That's right. Thank you for reminding me. Yes, I'll be going back soon."

Chapter Seven

Lyn, he's gorgeous."

"I think so, too." Carefully the blond woman lifted her tiny baby out of his bassinet and eased him against her breast. His eager lips sought her nipple and he suckled, content.

Skye laughed. "Now there's a man who knows what he wants." She had come down to the settlement as soon as she'd learned that Lyn was home from the hospital, and she was glad to see her friend able to move about so soon after the difficult birth. She was also hoping, she admitted to herself, that talking to her dearest friend would help her to clarify her own confused feelings about Cole Denton.

She'd tossed and turned most of the night after their abruptly terminated lovemaking. Her body had felt tense and aroused, and her mind had been racing with the implications of what they'd almost done. She had so wanted to give herself to Cole; what she felt for him surpassed anything she'd ever experienced in her life. But some instinct of self-preservation warned her to be cautious. If this man loved her and then left her, she sensed that she'd be a long time getting over the effects of it.

"Skye, is something wrong?"

With a start she turned back to her friend, blank eyes indicating that the question hadn't sunk in.

"I said, is something wrong? You've been miles away ever since you came down. And that's just not like you."

"Oh, Lyn. I don't know what to do." She twisted at a long strand of hair absently. "I'm falling for Cole Denton," she said. "Falling pretty hard."

"Good!"

"What do you mean, good?"

The blond woman laughed. "Skye, in all the years I've known you, you've never fallen for anyone. You've always been cool, always had the upper hand. That's why you've never gotten married, I think; you never found anyone who could throw you for a loop. It's good for someone like you to lose control every now and then."

"But what will happen when he leaves?"

Lyn shook her head in silent commentary as she shifted the now-asleep baby from her breast, and closed her blouse. With the bassinet in her other hand, Lyn led the way out of the house to the front porch. Once they were settled on the porch swing she lay the bassinet at her feet and said, "Still focused on the future instead of the present? I don't think Cole Denton is the kind of man who'd leave you heartbroken. You'd work something out."

"You should have heard him the other night," Skye said. "Talking about the way he needed to get back to the city." Unconsciously she pushed at the porch swing, making it move back and forth. "I just don't think it'll work. We're too different."

"Well, here comes someone who'll be glad to hear that," Lyn said, nodding down the street as she cradled the baby in her arms.

It was Tom. Skye sighed as she looked at him. She didn't really want to talk to Tom and see his wistful eyes. But she had to be kind to him; he'd been a good friend to her for many years.

"Hi, Tom," they chorused as he reached the sidewalk in front of Lyn's house.

"Hi, Lyn," he said. He gave Skye a cold glare and walked on.

"What's the matter with him?" she asked, surprised. She would have expected that sort of reaction right after she'd broken their unwritten engagement, but he had been friendly then. Now he seemed terribly angry at her.

"Maybe he's upset because Cole spent the night at your place after the day you were attacked."

"How does he know that? In fact, how do you know that?"

Lyn laughed shortly. "Oh, Skye. You know you can't hide anything in the settlement. Someone saw him coming down the next morning, and word spread."

"Oh, no." She turned to Lyn anxiously. "What are people saying about me?"

"Some are upset because he's an outsider. Because he's the big developer who's messing up our way of life, as they put it."

She nodded, frowning. She hadn't even considered that people might find out that he'd spent the night at her place.

"And of course Tom is jealous. He must be."

Skye twisted harder at her hair. "Lyn, he came up because he didn't want me to stay alone after what had happened with those three men that morning. And I let him stay—was glad to have him there, in fact. But we didn't sleep together."

"Why not?"

She looked at her friend, surprised by the question. "Well. . . ."

"Look, I asked because I assume you both wanted to. I wondered what stopped you, that's all. But if you don't want to talk about it, I understand." She reached out and took Skye's hand away from her hair. "And stop twisting your hair, for pete's sake. You haven't done that for years."

The tension was broken, and Skye grinned at her friend. "Thanks, Mom," she said dryly. She hesitated, not sure of how much to tell Lyn. "I did want to sleep with Cole. But . . . that wouldn't be enough for me. And that's all he can offer."

"You want true love, right?"

Skye flushed. "I guess it sounds kind of corny. But I think I'm falling in love with him. And it would hurt all the more if we'd made love, and then he left."

"I think you've already fallen, Skye," Lyn said, putting the baby down into its bassinet.

"Already fallen?"

"In love! Gracious, woman, you can be pretty thick headed for such a smart one." She turned to her friend. "Just listen to yourself. You've never agonized over a man before. You've never worried and gotten nervous like this." She held up her hand and assumed a solemn expression. "I detect love in the air."

Skye shook her head, laughing. "Let's change the subject. You should be getting back to bed to rest. And I'll watch the baby."

"Did you bring me some of your chamomile tea?"

"I sure did. So go fix yourself a cup and get to sleep." She stood and lifted the baby into her arms. "Little Joshua and I will start getting to know each other."

After Lyn was settled in bed with a cup of tea, Skye wandered back out onto the porch with the baby. She sat down on the porch swing, cradling him in her arms and crooning a soft, wordless tune to quiet it. She loved babies—and she'd always expected to have a family of her own. But now that Cole Denton had stepped into her life, her perspective had changed.

Before he'd come to the mountain she'd always expected, in the back of her mind, that she'd end up marrying Tom and living at a house in the settlement. Her life would be a lot like Lyn's; she would have two or three children and take care of them, living in some poverty but grateful for the strong community of the mountain to make life easier.

But in one short month Cole Denton had changed all that. After the emotional intensity she'd had with Cole, she knew that she couldn't possibly marry Tom and live the life of the settlement. Cole had taught her that there was a higher level of love, and now she wasn't willing—or even able—to settle for less.

She sighed, staring off down the dirt road absently. If Cole had been willing to stay on the mountain with her, his coming and awakening her to the larger joys of love would have been a blessing. But as it stood, she wished with all her heart that he'd never shown her how much she could feel. Because he would leave, and she would be here for the rest of her life—either as an old maid, or as an unhappily married woman who knew that there was more, somewhere, but had no chance of obtaining it.

The baby tried to suck at her breast through the shirt, and she laughed. "I'm not your mama, little boy," she said, hoping he wouldn't start to cry and wake up Lyn. But he wasn't really hungry, and soon he nestled back into her arms sleepily.

Maybe she should let things with Cole progress naturally, she thought. Then she would at least have memories after he left. It would be painful to have him leave her; but then, she reflected, it was painful now. She was depriving herself of him even while he was here. Perhaps she would regret her caution after he was gone.

Lost in thought, she leaned her head back against the porch swing and swung, lazily, crooning to herself as much as to the baby.

"You look good like that. With a baby."

She sat up abruptly, careful even in her surprise to keep little Joshua still. "Cole!" she said. "You surprised me."

He was dressed, as usual, in casual work clothes. His dark hair shone like onyx in the sun, and his gray eyes were warm as he looked down at her and the child. She found herself studying every line in his deeply tanned face in the hopes of remembering it vividly after he was gone.

"I'm surprised to see you, too," he said, sinking down onto the porch steps at her feet. "I had to come up this way to check on one of my workers who hurt his hand yesterday at the site, so I thought I'd look in on Lyn and the baby."

"Lyn's sleeping," she explained. "And Joshua and I are getting to know each other."

As if to prove the truth of her words, the baby nuzzled her breast again. "He keeps hoping I'm his mama," she said, laughing.

"You like kids, don't you?"

She nodded. "Love them. I'd like to have a dozen of my own, someday."

"Hope you've got a lot of energy," he said. "Big families are a handful."

"But the kids in a big family are never alone. They always have someone to turn to in hard times." Then she flushed. There was no point in talking about families with Cole; he didn't want to tie himself down, and he might think she was hinting at it. Determinedly, she changed the subject. "How's work at the site going?" she asked.

"Quite well. In fact, another week and the major construction will be completed."

She swallowed the lump that rose automatically to her throat and bent over the baby so he couldn't see her eyes. "Will you be leaving then?" she asked in a carefully neutral voice.

"Probably so. I'll have done all I came to do."

And more, she thought miserably. *You probably didn't plan to break a heart.*

"In fact," he continued, "I'm glad I saw you. I was going to come up later."

She waited.

"I wanted to ask you to go on a picnic with me on Saturday."

Conflict flared immediately within her. Should she avoid any more contact than necessary with him, in the hopes that her heart would be spared some pain? Or should she seize the opportunity to spend a few final hours with him? But even as she considered the options, she knew which one she would choose. "A picnic sounds like fun," she said.

"It's going to be a company picnic," he explained. "A kind of celebration now that the project's almost done.

We'll go to the reservoir for the day, with food and beer on Denton Row. It's been a tough job, and the men need some sort of reward."

The creak of the screen door announced Lyn's presence. "Mr. Denton! This is a surprise," she said.

"I came to check up on you and this little fellow. But I see now that you both look great."

Lyn was still rubbing her eyes. "I heard you spent the other night up at Skye's place," she said. "That was nice of you, some of us thought. To protect her and all. We worry about her up there alone."

Skye's face went scarlet. What was Lyn doing? She couldn't meet Cole's questioning glance.

"Oh, it wasn't Skye who told me," Lyn said, catching the question in Cole's eyes. "She's always more close-mouthed than most of us who live around here. But folks saw you coming down from her place the next morning." She smiled brightly at him, ignoring the horrified looks Skye was shooting her way. "No use trying to keep anything to yourself up here. The word spreads fast about things, especially when Skye's involved."

"I, ah, didn't realize people kept that close of an eye on each other."

"That's because you're from the city," Lyn said knowingly, taking the baby from Skye's arms. "Things are different here."

"I see," he said dryly. "Well, I'd best be getting back to work. Skye, tell Lyn about the picnic Saturday. Although I'm sure she'd hear about it soon enough, the way news travels."

Skye could only nod, but Lyn waved cheerily at Cole as he headed down the sidewalk. "See you later, Mr. Denton."

As soon as he was out of earshot, Skye turned furiously to her friend. "How could you have said that to him?" Her hands were on her hips, her whole body tense.

"What do you mean?" Lyn asked, an innocent expression on her face. "Oh, look. I'd better change him. Could you bring me out a diaper?"

Skye banged into the house, grabbed a diaper from the stack on the cabinet, and stormed back out. She thrust it at Lyn. "Here. Now don't try to change the subject again. Why did you say those things?"

"Oh, darn it. Now I need a wet cloth. Would you mind...?"

Rolling her eyes, Skye marched inside again, rummaged through Lyn's linen cupboard for a cloth, and dampened it in the cracked sink. She marched out again. "Here."

"Oh, look out!"

Skye stepped hastily out of the way.

"What bad manners, Joshua," Lyn scolded, then laughed. "Little girls don't have that kind of aim." She began to wipe the baby's bottom with the rag.

"I suppose you want some powder now."

"Well, I didn't want to ask, but..."

Sighing, Skye headed inside yet again, located the baby powder, and brought it back out onto the porch, letting the door bang shut behind her. She waited while Lyn powdered the baby, then pinned a clean diaper on him.

"Give me the dirty diaper. I'll put it in the pail."

"Thanks," Lyn said sweetly, a hint of a devilish smile shading her eyes and the corners of her mouth.

When Skye finally emerged from the house again, Lyn was putting Joshua down into his bassinet. "Was there something you wanted to ask me, Skye?"

"You know darn well what I wanted to ask! How could you have told Cole that you heard he'd spent the night at my house?"

Lyn sank down onto the porch swing next to her. "I was just trying to help, honey," she said.

"How was that helping? Letting him know what a bunch of small-town gossips are in the settlement?"

Lyn draped an arm around her shoulders. "Look. I knew it was going to make you mad. But I wanted to let Mr. Denton know what he was doing to you."

"What's that?"

"Skye, people are talking about you. No matter what happened, or didn't happen, that night at your place, people think you and Mr. Denton are lovers. And that's going to be hard for you when he's gone."

"No kidding. But why..."

"I think he's a decent man at heart. He just doesn't realize what he's doing to your reputation. When he realizes it, I think he's going to do the right thing by you."

"That's just what I don't want!" Skye burst out.

"You don't?" Lyn looked blank.

"I don't want him to marry me out of a sense of obligation. In fact, I don't even know if I'd want to marry him. We haven't gotten anywhere near the subject."

Lyn smiled. "I'll bet you do now."

"I don't want to," Skye said, lacing her hands together. "I know you meant well, but I wish you hadn't said anything. Cole's a big-city bachelor. Trying to tie him down would send him running."

"Maybe at first, but he'd come around. They always do."

"Not him." Skye shook her head. "There's something too...too careful about the way he treats me. It's as if he's afraid to get too close. And I don't want to put any demands on him if that's how he feels."

"Whatever you say, hon. But I think you're playing it too cool. He may not even realize that you care about him."

Skye thought of the times she'd come together with Cole in a hungry embrace. He knew her response to him, at least; that much was certain. But Lyn could be right that he didn't know of her growing emotional attachment to him. On the other hand, maybe that was good; nothing would be worse than to have him find out her feelings and make a half-hearted attempt to commit himself to her out of a sense of obligation.

No. It was best for both of them if her own increasing love for him was kept under wraps.

Forcing her mind back to present business, she concentrated on telling Lyn about the company picnic.

"That sounds fun," Lyn said. "I'll bet Mr. Denton will pull out all the stops and provide a great spread. He seems like the type who can be generous with his workers."

Skye nodded. "Are you going to feel well enough to come out by Saturday? You should still be taking it easy, you know."

"Well, I doubt if I'll be playing softball or volleyball. But I'm perfectly able to come and sit in a lawn chair and watch the other people play. Like an old lady."

Skye laughed. "You'll never sit still like an old lady. Not with your devilish ways. I'll bet you find out more gossip at this picnic than I've heard in the past year!"

The blond woman shook her head. "No. I'm not going to listen to just general gossip. I'm going to watch the way you and Mr. Denton act together. This is the kind of occasion where a romance can be made or broken. And I'll be there to see it all!"

Chapter Eight

Skye sat cross-legged on her bed, plaiting her still-wet hair into a long French braid. Sunlight streamed through the wide-open window, cooled by a gentle breeze.

A squawk at the windowsill caught her attention, though her hands never stopped their deft movements.

"It's a great day for a picnic, isn't it, Kronos?"

The crow squawked again in response, cocking its shiny black head.

"Just wait until I finish my braid, and I'll get you some bread." She slipped the elastic band onto the bottom of the thick braid and checked her handiwork in the mirror. The braid was smooth, and her bright sundress looked cheerful. "I'd better do something to my face to make it match the rest of me, right, Kronos?" she asked the crow. "I look like I'm going to a funeral instead of a picnic."

The crow hopped into the room and lighted on her dresser. It cocked its head to one side again as if considering her comment.

Clucking softly with her tongue, she brought her finger slowly to the bird's breast, and after a moment's hesitation he stepped onto it. "Good bird!" she said softly. "Now, let's go get you some bread." Talking softly to the bird the whole time, she carried it into the kitchen and let it rest on her shoulder while she sliced off a small chunk from the loaf. The crow grabbed eagerly at the bread as she walked to the door of the cabin and waited for it to fly off. The bird was so variable in its relationship with her; at times it seemed to remember the tender care it had received from humans in its infancy, and then it was practically fearless; at other times, its wild instincts seemed to reassert themselves and the bird could hardly be persuaded to get near a human being.

But this was one of Kronos's friendly times, and he stayed next to her as he pecked feverishly at the bread.

She wandered back inside after a moment, and the small statuette that Cole had bought her caught her eye. She picked it up, her fingers passing over the smooth contours. It would be all she had left of Cole in a few short days.

For a brief moment she had a vision of the years ahead of her: the settlement medicine woman, growing less and less needed as people learned to take advantage of the hospital and the new clinic, growing older alone in her cabin, with one tiny statuette to remind her of the brief period when her world had expanded and become meaningful under the warmth of Cole's attention.

This was the last day she would see him. The last time she'd ever look into the gray eyes and feel his hands touching her. Her throat constricted, and she hastily put the statuette down. She refused to waste time feeling sorry for herself. Quickly she grabbed her bag and went outside to wait for Cole on the porch.

She'd agreed to help him set up for the picnic, and she hoped it hadn't been a mistake. It meant that they would have time alone together, and that could be difficult. She was still torn between wanting to give as much of herself as possible to Cole, making their last hours together powerful, and backing away from him in an attempt to save her heart.

Absently she held out her hand to Kronos again when she realized that he'd flown down to the step beside her. This time he stepped fearlessly onto her finger and even allowed her to stroke his breast lightly. She clucked at him and he squawked in response.

"Sometimes I think you're part animal, Skye."

At the sound of the male voice, Kronos flapped off to the limb of a nearby tree. He squawked his displeasure at the interruption, and Cole winced.

"Sorry, buddy. But I have to take your girl away." He turned to her then. "I like your hair like that," he said, holding out his hand to her. "Are you ready to go?"

She nodded. As they jolted down the mountain road in Cole's truck, she studied him with sidelong glances. He was dressed in casual jeans and a gray knit shirt the color of his eyes, and his muscular frame was displayed to great advantage as he competently maneuvered the road's sharp turns. When he smiled over at her, his eyes crinkled appealingly and Skye felt her heart melt. He was so dear to her!

Once they reached the reservoir, however, such thoughts were pushed from her mind. The scene was hectic as they set out trays of food over troughs of ice.

Skye raised her eyebrows when she saw the three kegs of beer. "That's a lot of beer, isn't it?"

Cole laughed. "It'll be gone by the end of the afternoon, believe me. My men work hard, but when the work is done they like to play hard, too."

They were done with most of the setting up in good time, and Cole beckoned to her. "Come on. Let's go for a walk. The caterers can finish up, and people won't start arriving for half an hour or so."

He took her hand as they reached the edge of the forest, and the bittersweet emotions produced by his closeness were almost too much for Skye to handle. Try as she might, she couldn't focus only on the present; the bleakness of her future without him kept intruding. He seemed to sense her mood and was quiet as they walked along.

When they came to a small clearing that held an outcropping of rock, they paused as if by mutual assent. Skye perched on the largest rock and Cole sank down beside her.

"I've been thinking about something," he said, a trace of hesitation in his voice.

She met his eyes, waiting.

"Is it true what Lyn said? That everyone at the settlement knows I spent the night up at your place?"

She nodded. "I'm afraid so," she said. "People do tend to gossip an awful lot around here, because we've all known each other all of our lives."

"That bothers me. I don't like the idea of people talking about you in that way."

"Cole, it's nothing you need to worry about. It will blow over when some new scandal comes along."

"But that's just it. They're talking about us as a scandal, and it hardly seems fair when we haven't . . . well, consummated our affair."

She flushed, then forced herself to laugh. "Gossip isn't fair. But it's not a big deal. I wish Lyn had never mentioned it."

"I'm glad she did. Because it gave me an idea."

She picked at the green moss that clung to the side of the rock. She could hardly breathe.

He pulled her hands away from the rock and clasped them in his. "Come away with me, Skye."

Her heart pounded. What was he saying? On what terms? She felt ready to explode with questions, but her voice didn't seem to work.

She tried to pay attention to what he was saying.

"You see, I'd been looking at the situation from my point of view. I know a relationship like ours can't be permanent." He paused.

Skye let out her breath all at once and ducked her head to hide the expression on her face.

"Isn't that right?" he gently touched her chin, trying to make her lift her head.

But she couldn't, because she didn't want him to see the tears that were welling up in her eyes.

"Skye?"

Finally she nodded, her head still lowered. "I know it won't last," she whispered.

He was silent for a long moment, and when he finally did speak his voice sounded odd. "But there's always the philosophy that says to live for the moment. You could come away with me now, let me help you get your start in the city. Once you're on your feet and ready to stand alone, you could do it."

She kept blinking, willing the tears to go away. He was holding out the thing she wanted most in the world—the chance to be with him—and yet his eventual rejection was implied in the very invitation.

"I'm only offering because I see now how bad our relationship has looked to all the people here," he said. His voice still sounded odd to her, but maybe that was because she kept having to swallow so hard. "Skye, you have got to get out of this community. It's too small, too closed for you. If I can be the one to help you do that..."

Now he sounded like he was offering a public service. This was getting worse by the second. She wanted to press her hands over his mouth, to stop the words that kept coming out.

"Skye?"

She couldn't look at him.

"Dammit, woman, say something to me! Tell me that I'm not imagining what there is between us. If we went away together, away from all these prying eyes, I'd make it beautiful for you. Oh, Lord, Skye, I've been so hungry for you ever since I met you. I look at you and I go to pieces. I want to take you with me, to have you all to myself and taste all your sweetness. I want to teach you about love..." He paused. "How does that sound to you, Skye?"

She kept her head down. "Not so good," she said, low.

He was silent for a moment. "I know I'm a lot older than you are, and I can't offer the kind of life that one of your mountain men could—"

She stood up abruptly. "Forget it, Cole." She didn't want to hear him make excuses. It was plain what he thought of her: she was worth a few months of pleasure, but he was completely unwilling to make a long-term commitment. Blindly she headed back toward the picnic site, and was relieved when he didn't follow.

Just before she got back to the field where the tables were set up, she stopped and ducked off the path into a tiny copse of bushes. She couldn't face the people who were starting to trickle into the picnic area—not yet.

She sank down to the ground and wrapped her arms tightly around her knees, rocking back and forth. She'd thought she hurt before. But now it was worse; she'd been offered the chance to be with Cole, but only for a short while. He didn't think her worthy of marriage, that was plain; he wanted her only for her young body. He'd practically come out and said that she wasn't good enough for him in the long run.

And his offer wasn't even based completely on his desire for her. He'd felt obligated. In fact he'd said he hadn't even thought of it until Lyn's comment the other day about how people were talking. It was a great combination of reasons for wanting her to come with him, she thought bitterly: lust and obligation.

She tried to work up a strong, bracing anger against him. He had a lot of nerve treating her like she was easy. He should have realized that she wasn't the kind of woman who would just go away with a man for a few fun times, then move on.

But it was hard to feel angry at him. She kept thinking of his tenderness, his warm eyes. Maybe he was used to women who would be willing to do such a thing. Maybe she was just being old-fashioned.

Maybe she should take him up on his offer. She paused, horrified and yet fascinated by the thought. It would be a chance to be with him; it would put off the moment of parting a little longer. She could pretend that they were married, that he really loved her....

She hugged her knees tighter. It was a daring thought. But why not? What was waiting for her here? She remembered her earlier vision of her lonely future on the mountain and shuddered.

Suddenly a vision of Gran's face flashed before her eyes. It was so real, she gasped.

"What should I do, Gran?" she whispered, shutting her eyes as she visualized the woman's face. "Should I go with him or stay on the mountain?"

The words her grandmother would have said popped immediately into her mind, clear from all the times she'd asked Gran similar questions. "Think about how it would feel, honey," Gran would have said. "Would you feel happy and right inside if you did it, or not? That will tell you which is the right thing to do."

Still keeping her eyes tightly closed, she imagined what it would be like to be in Denver with Cole. He probably had a nice big home there. She could live there with him. Their nights together would be fantastic, that was certain; her body tingled at the thought of lying wrapped in his arms. The warmth, the tenderness he had to offer would be wonderful.

They would get up together in the mornings and she would cook his breakfast. And then he would go off to his job, and she....

She would do what?

Skye frowned as the image broke down in her mind. What would she do all day in Denver while Cole went to work? She could sketch, maybe; but since her inspiration came mainly from the world around her, the nature sketches probably wouldn't come easy in the city. She could go to school...but her heart sank at the memory of what it had been like to attend school in the city before.

And what would she do for friends? Cole might have friends he could introduce her to. They would probably be older, sophisticated people. She imagined the situation vividly. She and Cole would be standing together in the house, and the doorbell would ring. "Hello, Sam, Susan," Cole would say. "This is my..."

Lover? Little hick from the mountains?

She could imagine the expressions on the friends' faces. Pity. Contempt. She could imagine how sick she'd feel inside trying to fit into his crowd.

And worst of all...she envisioned waking up next to Cole one morning. "About time you'll be wanting to go back to the mountain, eh?" he would say. She imagined packing her bags and returning to her cabin. Greeting all her friends again, and seeing the sympathy or scorn in their eyes. And Cole would wave, and drive away.

With a shudder she opened her eyes and rubbed them, trying to dispel the images. How horrible. She would be an object of pity, and people would tell their daughters about her, about how she'd gone away with a city man, and come home in disgrace.

If she refused his offer and let him go now, at least she would have her self-respect. At least she'd be able to look her friends in the eye. And maybe, someday, she'd find a man who could make her forget Cole's gray eyes and tender touch.

In her heart, she knew she never could. What she felt for Cole would never be duplicated. She loved him more than she loved her own self. But she wouldn't degrade that love by letting their relationship take the route Cole was suggesting.

She stood up and smoothed out her braid. As she brushed the pine needles and dust from her sundress, she saw Cole passing down the path, heading back for the picnic. Briefly she wondered what he'd been doing all the time she'd been agonizing over her decision.

Probably, he's glad I told him to forget it, she decided. Now he wouldn't have the care of a country hick hanging over his head. Even though he desired her, she'd be too much trouble for a busy man like him. And he could still feel good about having fulfilled his obligation to her by offering to take care of her.

She held her head high as she emerged from the forest. And she continued to hold it high as she went through the motions of having a marvelous time at the picnic. She laughed with some of the workers who were cracking jokes. She admired the ample amount of food with Lyn and Bob. And she smiled broadly whenever Cole looked her way.

He seemed puzzled and distant. He spoke to her, but his eyes were veiled and he didn't seem to want to be near her for long. He was probably already forgetting about her, since she'd turned down his offer of a live-in affair; probably already thinking about the life he was about to return to in the city.

When everyone was done eating and was resting on the grass, most still drinking beer, Cole stood up.

"Speech, boss," one of the men called out, and others echoed the request.

Cole chuckled. "Okay, I'll make a speech. The best kind of speech."

"A short one?" someone yelled.

"That's right," Cole said. "I want to thank all of you who have stuck with us through a tough project. We have only one more week's worth of heavy work, and then it'll be on to something else for most of you. I want you to know that we appreciate the effort you've made and the job you've done for Denton Rec." He paused, his eyes scanning the assembled group of people. "And I'd especially like to thank you local people who've come in and worked with us. You've restored our faith in this community by the way you've worked hard, side by side with us."

Skye looked at Bob then, and noticed the faint flush of embarrassment on his face.

Cole went on. "I know it's been a difficult job in many ways, and you've had to contend with some heckling and some sabotage." A murmur went through the crowd. "And that's why I'm especially appreciative of your efforts. And that's also why—" he paused for a dramatic moment "—I want every bit of food and every drop of beer to be consumed before any of you goes home." He sat down amid laughter and applause.

Soon the group split off into different factions again. Some of the men set up a volleyball net, while others measured off a course for foot races. Skye stayed with Lyn, who sat holding her new baby on the grass.

"What's wrong between you and Cole?" the blond woman asked.

"You noticed."

"It's hard not to," Lyn said. "He keeps looking at you, but when you look back he turns away. Did you have a fight?"

Skye frowned. "Not exactly." She told Lyn of Cole's offer.

Lyn's eyebrows shot up. "You're kidding! Are you sure he meant it to be a temporary thing?"

"Positive. He said, and I quote, 'a relationship like ours can't be permanent.'"

Lyn shook her head. "Doesn't he realize that the scandal would be worse if you went and lived with him for a few months, and then came back to the mountain?"

"He thinks I should leave the mountain, anyway. It shows you he really doesn't know me very well. I don't want to leave, ever."

"Well..." Lyn paused. "To tell you the truth, I've never thought you'd stay here all your life. He could be right about you."

"You're crazy! Of course I'm staying."

"But if something important came along, a great job or a man you loved..."

"Maybe." Skye shifted impatiently. "But it's not going to be Cole Denton who takes me away. He wants a fling, nothing more, and he wants it away from the settlement and its gossip."

"So what did you say to him?"

"What do you think? I told him to forget it."

The blond woman shifted the baby in her arms. "I just don't understand it. I thought for sure he cared about you. I mean, more than just a short-term affair's worth."

Skye shrugged. "He's from the city, Lyn. He's used to having women around, dating and all, but he's not used to making commitments. We can't expect him to be the same as the men around here."

The crowd watching the foot races was getting more and more rambunctious, laughing and yelling as they watched the contestants run. The two women moved closer so that they could see the races.

Some of them were making an outright comedy of it; they'd had too much beer to drink, and their antics as they stumbled along were hilarious. Others took the races more seriously, especially after the winners of each two-man race started matching off.

"Look! It's Bob's turn," Lyn said, and they watched as he took his mark. He was one of the more serious ones. For a moment after his race started, he and the other man seemed to move at exactly the same pace, but as they neared the end of the course Bob pulled ahead.

"All right, Bob! That's one for the locals," Lyn called as he crossed the finish line. There was scattered clapping, but some of Cole's workers took mock offense.

"So it's the locals versus outsiders now, is it?" asked one burly man who'd won his first race. "Well, they call me Flash, and I'll take on anyone who thinks he's fast!"

Bob called out his willingness to race again, but he was still breathing hard from his last race. Another settlement man stood up. "I'll take you on, city slicker," he said, and the race was on.

This time, the burly man called Flash won, and the settlement people groaned. Skye looked around, surprised at the loudness of the sound, and realized that most of the picnickers had abandoned other pursuits and were watching the races.

Another settlement man who'd worked for Cole stood up to take on the challenge Flash threw out, but he lost, too.

"I guess you folks aren't as fast as you thought," Flash yelled, breathing hard.

"Take a break, man, and get your breath back," Bob said. "Then I'll take you on."

Flash nodded his agreement and flopped down on the grass, several of his co-workers surrounding him to offer advice and encouragement.

Skye grinned at Bob. "You'll beat him. I know how fast you are." She gestured toward the baby Lyn was holding. "Just think of Joshua there. Make him proud that you're his daddy."

"You ready, country boy?" Flash asked good-naturedly.

"I've been ready for a while. Just waiting for you." Bob rose smoothly to his feet and the two men bent at the starting line.

"Go!"

They were off, and immediately Skye and Lyn were on their feet, watching and hollering as Bob pulled ahead of the burly man. Bob was small, lean, and extremely quick, and he was developing a good lead.

When the two men were halfway through the course, Cole's workers started yelling encouragement to their man. The sound seemed to spur him on, and he started to close the distance between them.

"He's gaining on you, Bob!" One of the settlement people's yells penetrated the other noises, and Bob glanced back. In the instant that he looked away from the path in front of him, something made him lurch, then fall.

"He must have stepped in a hole," Lyn cried, and the other settlement people groaned as Flash finished easily.

Skye and Lyn hurried over to where Bob was sitting, rubbing his ankle. "Are you okay, hon?" Lyn asked, shifting the much-jostled baby on her arm.

"Yeah. Except for my ankle. And my pride. I could have beaten him!"

Skye squatted in front of him. "Let me see it," she ordered. She slipped off his tennis shoe and sock and probed the rapidly swelling ankle with skilled fingers.

"A sprain," she announced. "You'll have to stay off of it for a couple of days."

"Don't tell me one of my best workers is going to be out of commission? That's what I get for sponsoring a picnic. I should stick with being a slavedriver."

Skye looked up at the sound of Cole's voice. She hadn't known he was watching the race. Their eyes locked for a long moment. "I'm—I'm afraid he's going to have to take a day or two off," she said, trying to keep her tone light.

"With pay, of course," Lyn said, her voice filled with laughter. "After all, he was hurt in the line of duty."

"Lyn!" Bob scolded. "Of course not with pay."

"We'll see about that," Cole said.

Skye was still probing at Bob's ankle. "Does anyone have an ace bandage or something to wrap this up with?"

"I think there's a first-aid kit in the truck," Cole said, and was off in that direction. He returned quickly, waving the metal box.

Deftly Skye wrapped up the ankle, and Cole helped Bob to limp off the field.

Flash ambled over to the picnic bench where they'd deposited Bob. "Hey, man, are you all right?" he asked.

Bob nodded.

"That was tough luck," the burly man said. "But I guess that means the Denton workers win, huh? Unless the locals have another runner to put up."

"I guess so," Bob said. He turned to the small group of settlement people who had crowded around. "Sorry to let you down, folks."

"Wait a minute." Lyn stood up, hands on hips. "The fastest runner on the mountain hasn't even raced yet."

Bob frowned, clearly annoyed with his wife. "Who do you mean?"

"Skye Archer, that's who. She's been racing settlement men ever since she was a kid. And beating every one of them."

"Now, wait a—" Skye began.

But Bob's eyes had begun to dance. "That's for darned sure. She can beat all of us, hands down. How about it, Skye?"

Other settlement voices chimed in.

"Come on, Skye!"

"Race for us!"

"Don't let those city people beat us!"

But the man called Flash was frowning in disbelief. "You want to put a woman up? Against me?" He guffawed. "She wouldn't have a chance."

That decided her. "You may eat your words, big guy," she said, standing up next to him. He was a foot taller than she, and twice as big around, and he was shaking his head as he looked down at her.

"Look at how she's dressed," another Denton worker said. "She doesn't even have tennis shoes on."

Skye looked down at her sandals. "I'll run barefoot," she decided, and kicked them off. Running in a dress didn't faze her at all; she always wore dresses, but they were usually comfortable and non-constricting, and this one was no exception.

"Are you ready, Flash?" she asked, grinning at the burly man.

"If you say so, little lady," he said dubiously.

They took their places, and Skye considered the race ahead. This was a little different than her races down the mountain; in those, there was slyness involved in choosing what route to take. In this race, speed was more of a factor than intelligence, but she still felt confident that she could beat the big man beside her.

"On your mark!"

She assumed an easy starting position, only half-crouched, unlike the man beside her who was fully coiled down.

"Get set!"

She waited, emptying her mind of all distractions.

"Go!"

She was off! Legs pumping, braid flying out behind her, she ran joyously, swiftly, thoughtlessly. She had always loved to run, loved the sense of freedom and wildness that came with speed. Her legs flashed out in front of her, taking longer and longer leaps. Without thinking about it, she was aware of every bump and hole in the grassy field, and her bare feet found the smoothest path every time.

They were halfway there, and the burly man was right beside her. She was only dimly aware of him; he was simply a force to be beaten rather than a real person.

He edged ahead, and she heard, as if from a great distance, the disappointed shouts of the settlement people.

"Come on, Skye!"

"Don't let us down!"

She looked at the finish line and concentrated on it. She felt her speed increase without thinking about how she did it.

Dimly she saw herself draw even with the burly man again. The sound of his heavy breathing seemed far away.

"That's it, Skye!"

"Now you've got him!"

She heard his grunt of annoyance and watched out of the corner of her eye as he forced his muscles to carry him more quickly. He was straining hard, his face red, his breathing hoarse and heavy. She looked up toward the finish line again.

Just behind it was Cole Denton. He was grinning skeptically as he watched her run.

It was the impetus she needed. She'd show him! She drew a deep breath and let herself fly, completely free now as she sped past the gasping Flash and crossed the finish line a step ahead of him.

"You did it!" Bob cried as he slapped her shoulder. She bent down, catching her breath as she heard the babble of congratulations around her.

"That was amazing."

"Where'd she learn to run like that?"

She heard one of the settlement women explaining the traditional chase down the mountain to some Denton workers, and she stood up, frowning. She didn't want them laughing at mountain customs.

But her attention was distracted by Flash. "You beat me fair and square," the big man admitted, his breathing still labored. "I never would have guessed it would be a woman who brought me down."

She smiled sweetly at him. "Maybe you'll think twice before you challenge a woman again," she said.

His eyes were bright with admiration. "I wouldn't mind making a habit of challenging a woman like you," he said. "Does the loser get a kiss?"

"I didn't notice you kissing Bob when you beat him," she said tartly, and the surrounding group of people laughed. "But if you insist...." She reached up and planted a loud, smacking kiss on his cheek and then backed quickly out of reach.

"Hey, that's not the kind of kiss I—"

"Take what you can get and consider yourself lucky, Flash," Cole said. There was a note of annoyance in his voice.

Lyn stood up on the bench of a picnic table. "Well, I guess the locals won after all," she called out. "Country folks beat city folks!"

Flash held up a hand. "Don't lay this defeat on me alone, guys. Doesn't anyone want to take this little lady on?"

"Not in a race," one of the workers called out. "Now, if you wanted to talk about other things—"

"We're talking about racing," Cole said. "And that's all."

Skye looked around, her eyes sparkling with the excitement. "Aren't there any other challengers?"

"What about you, boss?" one of the Denton workers called out.

"Yeah, Cole."

"Take her on!"

"You can beat a woman, can't you?"

Cole looked over at her. His eyes were dark and unreadable, but a slow grin creased his face. "I don't know if I could beat such a fast one as that."

"Aw, come on, boss."

"Are you scared?" she asked him. Her heart was pounding as her eyes locked with his. This was one area where she was on equal ground with him, and the thought of a competition between them was exhilarating. She could beat him! She knew she could. Here, if nowhere else, he would have to realize that she was a force to contend with.

"Well..." Cole said, looking around at the assembled men.

"Do it!"

"Go ahead!"

He stood with his usual easy grace. "I believe I will," he said.

When he looked at her again, the challenge in his eyes, she felt her heart leap. He looked so confident, so...almost arrogant. Maybe he could beat her, at that.

"I don't know if I can do it, Lyn," she whispered to her friend.

"Of course you can! He's just acting cocky to shake you up."

"But he—"

"Remember how cocky Flash was?"

Lyn was right. Most men thought they were, by definition, stronger and faster than women. The men who used to chase her down the mountain had always expected to catch her at first; it had only been after repeated defeats that the settlement men had realized, one by one, that she was faster than any of them.

"Are you ready, lady? Or do you need to rest for a while?"

The challenge in Cole's voice spurred her. "Of course I'm ready. No problem here," she said in an elaborately casual voice.

As they took their places side by side at the starting line, Skye's heart pounded. The shouting voices grew faint in the background as she met Cole's gray eyes.

"Are you ready for the race of your life?" he asked her softly.

"You'd better believe it."

Someone came up to start them off while the majority of the crowd headed toward the finish line to see the race's final moments.

"On your mark!"

They took their positions. Once again Skye only crouched halfway, but Cole took a full racing position, poised on his hands and kneeling legs.

"Get set!"

Cole glanced over at her and flashed a grin of challenge. It did strange things to her heart, but her muscles ignored the twinges of excitement as they tensed for the takeoff.

"Go!"

They were off! Cole's crouched start got him a slight jump on her, but she closed it immediately. She gloried in the feeling of lithe speed, aware of nothing but her pounding legs and the man beside her. Even though she was a little tired from the previous race, she could tell that she was running faster now.

She remembered briefly the offer he'd made her that morning, and the blood pounded harder at her temples. So he thought she was a good-time girl and nothing more, did he? Well, she would show him now that there was some substance to her. She'd give him something to remember her by.

Her legs pumped harder and she watched out of the corner of her eye as she pulled ahead of him. *Come on, body,* she told herself. She inched further ahead.

Looking up, she could see the finish line just a short distance away. She would beat him! She felt a grin start to crease her face even as she ran with all her might.

The people's shouting grew louder. She was almost there! She was going to win!

Then it happened.

Out of the corner of her eye she saw Cole pulling even with her. Desperately she tried to summon more speed, but she was already expending every bit of might that she had.

The finish line was there! Could she still—

He pulled ahead.

She knew, even as she crossed the finish line, that he'd beaten her. By only a fraction of an inch, true, but he'd done it. Her head spun as she realized that Cole Denton was the first man, ever, who had beaten her in a race.

"It's a tie!"

"A tie!"

"No, Cole won. He pulled ahead at the last minute."

"Looked to me like the girl won."

She heard the shouts faintly, then focused on them as their import hit her. No one really knew what had happened. Her reputation was intact! She shot a covert glance at Cole, only to see him looking at her, eyebrows raised questioningly. One look at the triumph in his eyes told her that he knew he'd won.

She turned to the crowd and held up her hand, her breath still coming hard. "Folks, he beat me fair and square. It was close, but he went ahead in the last minute."

"Aw, Skye."

"Are you sure? It looked like a tie from here."

Cole stood up straight then, too. "It was a tie," he said.

She looked at him in surprise. Why was he lying? She knew that he'd realized his victory; it had been plain in his eyes.

One of the settlement men came and slapped Cole on the back. "You've done more than we ever were able to do, even by just tying with her."

Another man chimed in. "Yeah, that's right. None of us ever came close." He bent close to Cole and whispered something in his ear.

"Is that so?" Cole laughed loudly. "Well, we'll just see about that."

What had the man said? When she saw Cole's speculative gaze resting on her, she flushed and turned away. Despite the fun they'd had, there was still a major misunderstanding between them.

Lyn tapped her on the shoulder. "Well, what really happened? Did he beat you?"

Skye nodded. "I'm sure he did," she said. "I don't know why he's not claiming his victory."

"You know what this means."

"What?"

"Any man who can beat you gets to marry you, right?"

Skye stared at her friend as the words sunk in. "Lyn! What on earth—"

"The chase, silly. Aren't those the rules?"

Skye shook her head. "It's not the same at all. He's an outsider!"

Lyn laughed. "You just don't want to admit it to yourself, hon," she said, then turned her attention to her baby.

Skye stood stock-still, considering what Lyn had said. It was true, she supposed; if she was truly living by the old mountain traditions, then Cole would have the right to marry her since he'd beaten her in a race.

But he hadn't claimed his victory! He hadn't wanted to acknowledge that he'd won. Her heart plummeted as she realized why he had called the race a tie.

He hadn't wanted to marry her!

He knew the custom; she'd told it to him on the evening he'd gotten snowed in at her cabin. He knew that to beat her was, in mountain terms, to gain the right to have her as his wife. But he hadn't wanted that right! She shivered, suddenly cold, as she remembered his words in the forest that morning. He hadn't even mentioned marriage.

A lump rose to her throat, making it ache. The insult was subtle; probably no one else would recognize it. But to her it was a slap in the face. And more than that, it was a heartbreaker. She loved this man, and she wanted nothing more than to be with him for the rest of her life.

She studied him for a moment. He still stood at the center of a knot of Denton workers, grinning and nodding as they congratulated him. He was glorious. He stood half a foot taller than any of them, and his easy power was evident in the straight set of his back and the look of confidence on his face.

He caught her eyes then, and came over to her. "I have to work late at the trailer tonight," he said, referring to the makeshift office he had on the site. "But I'd like to see you before I leave town. Can I come up tomorrow afternoon?"

"Sure," she said. She couldn't hide the listlessness in her voice.

He looked at her, the smile vanishing from his face. "Two o'clock?"

As she nodded, she heard Lyn calling her. "I have to go," she said. Avoiding his eyes, she headed toward Bob and Lyn's pickup.

After Lyn and Bob had dropped her off in front of the store, she went numbly about the shopping she had to do. A cloud of despair had descended over her. He didn't want to marry her. He would be gone soon. Tomorrow would be her last chance to see him.

His face kept floating before her eyes, tormenting her. She loved him. Oh, how she loved him. And she had lost him.

"Skye. Hey, Skye!"

The voices belonged to two of the younger settlement men, and forcing herself to come out of her daze, she greeted them.

"Did you say goodbye to Cole Denton?" one of them asked. He was smiling as he shifted the heavy metal jug he was carrying from one hand to the other.

"Uh, sure." Did everyone know about Cole's rejection of her? Would people start to make fun of her?

"Good."

As they walked off, one of them mumbled something to the other, and they both broke out laughing. To Skye's ear the laugh had a mean sound, and it only depressed her more.

Maybe Cole and Lyn were right. Maybe the settlement was getting too small for her. She couldn't bear it if people were going to laugh at her because of what she'd felt for Cole.

Absently she picked up her groceries and headed up the mountain for home.

Chapter Nine

As she halfheartedly warmed up some soup for dinner, Skye felt something bothering her. Something hadn't seemed right, and she'd been too preoccupied with her own misery to notice it.

It was the two young settlement men. Their behavior had been strange, out of character. They were sometimes wild, but she'd never known them to be mean.

Times change and so do people. Skye smiled faintly, remembering Gran's familiar saying. It was true, the two of them might have changed; and she was probably overreacting to it.

She sat down, stirring the bowl of soup in front of her. She wondered what Cole wanted to talk to her about. Would he repeat his offer? For a moment she toyed again with the idea of taking him up on it. She didn't know if she could stand to live with the heavy, bleak sense of despair that gripped her whenever she thought of his leaving.

But moving in with Cole would only put it off and make it worse when they finally did break up for good. And she'd have lost her self-respect, as well. Better just to stand firm and say no.

She ate spoonfuls of the soup, then stared at it with distaste. Her stomach was churning so badly that she couldn't put another thing into it. She took the bowl out onto the porch and called Farimer, who panted ecstatically at his mistress's unusually generous offering.

When the dog was done lapping the bowl, she bent to pick it up. As she carried it back into the cabin, she shook her head. She was afflicted with a full-fledged case of depression, that was clear. It wasn't a familiar feeling. But then, she'd never been in love before. Nor had she ever been completely rejected.

As she rinsed the bowl, her thoughts returned to the settlement men in the store. Something in their behavior—or maybe it was in the way they looked—was tickling her intuition, but she couldn't pin it down.

She wondered if they were among the group that had sabotaged Cole's work all along.

Suddenly she stopped cold. What had they asked her? *Whether she'd said goodbye to Cole.*

Was there a hidden meaning behind that question? Could they be planning some final destruction at the site?

And then the dish dropped from her hands and crashed to the floor.

They'd been carrying *kerosene*!

And Cole was to be working late at the site tonight.

Ignoring the shards of crockery around her, she ran to her bedroom and threw on socks, shoes, and a dark jacket. An instant later she was banging out of the cabin, flashlight in hand. Why hadn't she ever bought a car?

She ran down the trail, years of familiarity coming to her aid in the thick darkness. She was breathing hard, her heart pounding as visions of Cole caught in the trailer in flames flashed through her mind.

She ran faster. What if she was too late? What if they had already—

Forcing the thought out of her mind, she concentrated on the trail in front of her. Dark shapes rose before her, menacing, but she kept going recognizing them belatedly as trees and rocks.

The lights of the settlement blazed to her left, and she paused momentarily. Should she stop and get help? But there wasn't time to convince anyone that one of their neighbors was planning something so horrendous. There simply wasn't time. She hurried past the settlement, and the path grew dark again as the lights faded behind her.

The darkness grew even thicker as she entered the pine forest near the bottom of the mountain, and Skye, who'd never been afraid of the dark as a child, found herself jumping at each little noise she heard. The flashlight's beam seemed weak and thin, rendering only a few feet in front of her light. She was forced to slow down to a walk to avoid tripping over rocks and roots.

She heard a crashing sound in the distance behind her. What was it? Walking faster, she tried to ignore the sound. It was probably some animal, a squirrel or rabbit.

She scanned the sky ahead, looking for signs of fire at the site. But the darkness was unbroken and she felt relieved. She was fairly certain that she would have been able to see a fire from here if there was one.

The crashing sound behind her grew louder. No squirrel or rabbit could make that kind of noise. She quickened her pace, scanning her mind for the nocturnal animals who might make such a noise.

A wolf? A mountain lion? She walked faster still.

The crashing behind her grew louder.

Or a man? Her eyes widened in panic. What if it was another vacationer with evil on his mind? What if it was the men with the kerosene, crazed with a desire for revenge and aware that she was going to try to stop them?

She started running. Her breath was coming hard as she heard the bushes crashing behind her, branches breaking, rocks falling. What would make such noise?

The crashing was right behind her now. She sped up, running frantically in the darkness. The exposed root seemed to come out of nowhere.

She fell, crashing to the ground, the flashlight flying away into the brush beside the path. A dark shape loomed over her. She tried to scream, but no sound came out.

She shut her eyes and waited.

Something wet brushed over her face. A familiar smell. A familiar whine.

"Farimer!"

The dog raced around at the sound of her voice, pinning her playfully at the shoulders with his massive paws, then bounding off in circles around her. Her pulse rate slowed back down to normal and she sat up, brushing the dirt and sticks off of her clothes and out of her hair.

"Farimer, you bad, bad dog," she scolded, standing up. "You made me lose my flashlight."

The dog ignored her scolding tone, continuing to run joyously around her. He seemed to think this was a pleasure trip.

A pleasure trip! Exactly what it wasn't. She had to hurry.

"Come on, boy. You'd better stay with me." She turned and continued down the path. If only she'd had the presence of mind to hold on tightly to that flashlight. Now she had to pick her way slowly. Would she make it in time?

Cole sat in his trailer office, the financial reports for the project spread out in front of him. He had a ton of paperwork to finish before they closed down this stage of operations next week.

But he was having a hard time focusing on the charts in front of him. A dark-haired, slender woman kept springing into his mind, blocking out the papers.

He remembered the race, and a slow smile crossed his face. He'd beaten her, but only by a few inches. And she'd been running barefoot. The girl was incredibly fast.

What was it she had told him once about the traditional chase down the mountain? "If a man could catch me, he'd probably make a good husband and father." Something like that. He wondered if she'd thought about the race today in the same context.

No. Probably not. She'd seemed appalled at the thought of even living with him; marriage was out of the question.

He wasn't exactly surprised at her reaction. Young women today didn't want to settle down early; he knew that. They had multiple options before them and they wanted to seize them. They wanted excitement and individuality and variety. Deidre had taught him that.

After all, she was still practically a girl; he, on the other hand, was thirty-five. He was probably too old and stodgy for her. Impatiently he raked his hands through his hair, feeling morose.

She probably thought of him more as a father figure than as a lover.

Then he shook his head. She hadn't reacted to him like a father. He felt a tightening in his groin as he remembered the night they'd spent together after the incident with the three attackers. A vision of her naked breasts flashed before his eyes, and he felt his mouth go dry. Skye was innocent, but there was a sensuality in that soft body that was just waiting for someone to awaken it.

He ran a hand over his head distractedly. He wanted to be the one to do that, dammit. He wanted to marry her, to spend the rest of his life with her.

He considered her youth again. Funny how little difference it made from his point of view. There was an ageless quality about the woman that kept her from seeming immature. She had more interests than many people twice her age. With her healing talents, her wide reading, her art—and her love—a man could rest content forever.

Shaking his head, he leaned over his papers again. He ought to stop thinking about what couldn't be. She'd seemed sad but sure that she wouldn't even consider his offer; it was crazy to even think about repeating it tomorrow.

But he had to. He had to at least try once more. If he could talk her into spending a few months with him, he'd at least have the memories to live on after she'd left.

It wasn't enough, but it was better than nothing.

He forced his attention back to the work before him. These reports would stay here until he completed them; he was the boss, and the buck stopped with him.

A faint shuffling noise penetrated his consciousness a few minutes later. Cole brushed it aside without giving it any thought. His pencil continued to move over the long columns, filling in figures.

The shuffling continued, accompanied now by some soft thuds and bangs. The noise penetrated his thoughts slowly and he wondered whether raccoons had found their way into the site.

He got up and peered out the trailer's small window. And froze.

There were two men out there. No, three. He recognized them slightly, having seen them around town. What were they doing here, sneaking around after dark?

Cole switched off the desk lamp in the trailer so that he could see the men more clearly. They were creeping around, each carrying something bulky, but the clouds over the moon made the night too dark to make out what they were doing.

They had to be saboteurs. And this was his chance to catch them in the act. Cole grinned to himself. No one would expect a construction boss to work late hours in an office. These scoundrels obviously thought they had the place to themselves. They weren't even trying to be particularly quiet.

The shortest man came closer. He was making strange gestures with the dark object in his hand, and Cole wondered if they were signals to the other partners.

As the man continued his odd motions, a dark shape came out of the surrounding darkness. But it wasn't human. It was a giant, dark dog, bounding up toward the man, leaping at him with excessive friendliness.

Wasn't that Skye's dog? What the hell was her dog doing on the site at this time of night?

He peered into the darkness again, and his heart jumped. There, emerging from the obscurity into the dim light cast by the men's lantern, was Skye.

She glanced toward the trailer, then away. She was heading straight for the two men nearest her, and they were watching her come.

Had they planned this? Could it possibly be that Skye, the woman he'd trusted and—who was he kidding?—had come to love, was in league with the saboteurs?

He had thought so at first, he remembered. She was so fiercely loyal to the settlement and its people. He remembered how opposed she had been to change on the mountain, how angry at Denton Rec. Could she still be looking for revenge?

But he couldn't believe it of Skye. He thought of her dark, liquid eyes that had looked at him so lovingly. There was no way that she would try to hurt him. Was there?

He frowned and shifted his weight to a more comfortable position as he continued to crouch at the darkened window. What was she doing there, then? She knew he was planning to work late; he'd told her that, and the way she'd looked over at the trailer made him suspect that she was checking to see if he was there.

Had she come to warn the men of his presence? Was she worried that they would be caught?

Was she in love with one of them?

The thought of Skye with another man sent a sharp stab of pain through his heart. Most of the men here simply weren't good enough for her. They wouldn't help her to develop all the talents and skills that were a part of her. An image of one of these men putting his rough hands on Skye's body made him cringe physically, and his fists clenched.

It didn't help to see Skye come up to the shortest man and touch his arm.

Cole strained to hear what they were saying to each other, but he was too far away and no words were distinguishable. All he heard was a low murmur. He was forced to rely on body language to interpret what was going on between the two of them.

He watched as Skye gestured toward the dark object in the man's hands, then over toward the trailer. She seemed to be asking him or telling him to do something.

The man shook his head vigorously. She touched the object in his hand, and he jerked it away. He motioned her off toward the darkness from whence she'd come.

Grabbing at his hand, she tried to pull him along with her, away from the site into the darkness. But he jerked away and started making those strange motions again.

Cole let out his breath in a soft sigh. He hadn't even been aware that he was holding it. From what he could see, it looked like Skye was trying to dissuade him from whatever he was doing. The other two had come up briefly, then gone back to what they were doing.

What *were* they doing? Cole tried to identify those gestures the men kept making. What were they? It was almost as though they were throwing something out of the object, as if it were a container of some kind....

Even as the thought broke through his mind, he smelled it. Of course! It was kerosene!

And he could smell it here, by the trailer.

He started toward the door, then paused. Cool was the way he had to play it here. Because one match, lit by any one of them, could send the whole site up in flames.

Moving slowly and quietly, he eased open the door of the trailer. Skye's gestures and motions were getting more frantic now. Obviously the men weren't doing what she wanted them to do. She grabbed hold of one man's arm again and tried to pull him away.

He flung her off, and she fell to the ground. Cole felt a slow rage start to build inside him. Whatever his gripe with Denton Rec, this man had no right to treat her like that. Stealthily he crept toward the pair.

The man tossed aside the dark object, and the clang it made as it banged against some rocks confirmed what Cole had been virtually certain of before. It was a kerosene jug. But there was no time to feel self-congratulatory about guessing right. Because the youngest man was going for something in his pocket, and Cole felt a sinking certainty about what it was going to be.

He headed toward the group, his footsteps noiseless. He saw Skye start to rise from where she'd fallen, her eyes never leaving the youngest man.

He proceeded to light a match.

"No! Don't do it! Please!" Her sudden screams startled the man, and he turned toward her. The gentle breeze fanned out the match.

Cole breathed a sigh of relief and continued to walk toward the group.

"Dammit, Skye. Get out of here. This is no place for you."

"Yeah, go on home." The two men who weren't lighting matches sounded more frightened than angry, and Cole guessed that Skye's presence had made them realize the enormity of what they were doing.

The man with the matches, though, wasn't frightened; he started to light a second one. This time Skye's screams didn't affect him.

When she realized that screaming hadn't worked, she scrambled toward him, and Cole had to bite down the urge to yell at her. There was no telling what this man could do to her; he was obviously unstable and violent.

As if to confirm that fact, the man started yelling. "Stay away from us! We're gonna do it no matter what you think! We're gonna get rid of Denton for good!"

The man held the match toward the dark pool of kerosene in front of him. Skye moved toward him, on her feet now, and for a moment Cole thought she meant to tackle the younger man. An involuntary flash of admiration went through him even as he cursed her foolishness.

She sat down in the puddle of kerosene.

Cole's eyes widened with disbelief.

"What the hell do you think you're doing?" the man roared. "Get out of there. You'll burn up!"

"No way, John. If you want to burn the site, you'll have to burn me, too."

"Are you crazy?" one of the other men said, sounding even more nervous than before. "Get on out of there."

Skye shook her head and sat motionless.

He let the match go out in an angry twitch of his fingers. "Damn you, woman! I'm not letting you ruin our plans!"

"Listen, you don't want to kill a man, do you? I'm telling you, Cole Denton could be in that trailer. If you set this place on fire, you'll fry him alive!"

Cole winced at her choice of words as he tried to position himself to his best advantage.

"Look at that trailer," one of the other men said. "It's dark. There's no one in there."

"And if there was," said the man with the matches, "it would be what he deserves for coming in here and ruining our lives."

"You're the only ones ruining your lives," she said. Cole marveled at how calm she was able to sound, sitting in the kerosene. The woman had guts, no doubt about it.

"Come on, Skye. Please get out of here." The man's voice had dwindled to a whine.

"Not until he gives me those matches."

The youngest man reached in his pocket and fumbled for something. But from Cole's vantage point, he could see that it wasn't matches. An instant later, the man's hand emerged with a flashing blade in it.

"Honey, I don't want to do this," he said. "But I will. Get out of here now." He advanced toward her with the blade flashing in his hand. The other men loomed menacingly behind him, backing him up.

"John, guys, it's me," she said, and for the first time he heard real fear in her voice.

"So be a good girl and go home."

She sat immobile, the men right next to her now. The one with the knife held it to her arm. "Move!" he ordered, his voice fraught with tension.

She didn't. From where Cole was, now right behind the group, he could see the tiny droplets of blood springing to life on her skin. She winced, but she stayed where she was.

At the sight of red blood on Skye's white skin, Cole's rigid control snapped. "Get away from her!" he roared as he charged the man with the knife.

The man turned, surprised, a snarl emerging from his mouth. But Cole had the advantage of surprise as well as size, and his flying tackle sent the younger man crashing to the ground. He was amazed at his own rage as he pinned the man, then stunned him with a crashing blow to his jaw.

Dimly he heard the sounds of running feet, and then he felt a light touch on his arm.

"It's okay now, Cole," Skye said, her voice soft. "The other two ran away, and I think this one's knocked out."

Chapter Ten

Where are you taking me?"

"You'll see."

Skye bounced impatiently on the seat of Cole's truck. He was being altogether too mysterious about this trip today.

"How's your arm?" he asked, changing the subject.

She passed a hand over the white bandage, grimacing at the reminder of last night's madness at the site. "It's going to be fine," she said. "It's just a surface wound."

They rode along the highway in silence, and as Skye gazed at the mountains that lined the left side of the road, she thought of the preceding night's events. She'd been terrified when she had seen those men with their kerosene jugs. Though the trailer's darkness had led her to hope that Cole had already left, she hadn't been quite sure. In her determination to save Cole and his work, she'd taken a big risk, and its implications had only struck her halfway to the sheriff's office.

She could have died. They all could have died. She let out a shuddering sigh at the memory.

"Thinking about last night?" Cole asked.

She nodded. "I wonder what will happen to them? I can still hardly believe they meant to burn the whole site down."

"I can," Cole said grimly. "I've seen what bitterness can do to people."

They rode on in silence, and Skye's thoughts drifted again. She wondered what Cole was planning. He'd come for her at two o'clock today and asked her to go for a drive. She could tell he was taking her someplace in particular because of the strange way he was acting.

And yet she couldn't figure it out. This was the last time they would see each other, if things went as planned; he was finishing up work at the site tomorrow and leaving tomorrow night. She couldn't imagine what sort of a surprise would be right for their last hours together.

But no matter what ended up happening, she was glad she'd known Cole Denton. She'd never forget him; in fact, she'd probably never get over him. Still, it was better to have loved and lost....

She sighed. What if he repeated his offer to have her move in with him again? It was so tempting. Last night, when she'd thought of him in mortal danger, she hadn't hesitated to risk her own safety for him. It had been a thoughtless, instinctual reaction, and that, more than anything else, had confirmed to her that she treasured him beyond anything else in her life.

She would even be willing to move to the city for him, she had concluded last night as she'd lain in bed, sleepless, after Cole had dropped her off. She would have moved to the city for him—if he had been willing to make a long-term commitment.

But he wouldn't. He'd shown the other day how completely opposed he was to the idea.

"Almost there," Cole said.

She looked around with renewed interest, sitting up straighter in the pickup's seat. They were heading up a mountain road, but to one side she could see the urban sprawl of Colorado Springs.

The road wound up the mountain. Now tall pines lined it, interrupted only occasionally by a small group of houses. The view of the city was gone now, except for occasional glimpses through gaps in the trees.

As they drove higher, the road grew rougher, and the number of dwellings decreased. The area started to look more wild.

"This is a beautiful place, Cole," she said.

He smiled in response, but she noticed that his knuckles were white on the steering wheel and his jaw was set. What was he so tense about?

"Here we are," he said, turning off the road onto a gravel driveway.

She glanced over at him again, struck by the strain in his voice. Then her attention was taken up by her surroundings. The pines were thick here, but there was a clearing ahead. As Cole pulled the truck forward, the most beautiful house she had ever seen came into view.

Its entire front was glass. The beams that supported the glass were natural wood stained a deep shade of brown, and the same shade was repeated over the rest of the house. Cunning landscaping made it impossible to tell where nature stopped and the man-made garden started, but there were cultivated flowers and bushes next to the large deck area.

She turned to Cole and found him studying her, watching her reactions.

"Cole, what—"

"Let's go inside," he said.

Was it his house? Why had he brought her here?

Inside she walked through the rooms, marveling at the unhampered view that most of them provided. The house was scantily furnished, but there was carpeting on the floors and the kitchen was fully equipped. It looked ready to move into, but clearly no one lived there now.

She sank down onto the stone hearth in front of a Franklin stove. "Cole, I won't budge another step until you tell me what this is all about," she said.

There was tension in his jaw again, although his voice, when he spoke, was lighthearted. "Do you like this place, Skye?"

"Of course I do. I love it."

"Good." He squatted down on the carpet, brushing at a tiny spot of dirt as if it held his full attention and was the most important thing in the world.

She exploded. "Cole Denton, you tell me right now why you're showing me this house, or I'll never speak to you again." Then she frowned as she realized that the threat didn't make much sense; after today, she wouldn't have the opportunity to speak to him again, most likely.

He looked up from the spot of dirt and met her eyes. "How would you like to live here?"

"What do you mean?" Was he repeating his offer of a temporary live-in arrangement? And how could she turn him down when he looked so anxious and pleading?

"I mean, would you like to live here with me?"

Her heart turned over. He *was* repeating his offer. And she didn't know if she had the strength to turn him down. She stared miserably into his gray eyes, drowning in them, unable to speak.

"Lord, woman, don't look at me that way," he said. He shifted into a sitting position closer to her and took her hand.

"For how long?" she asked.

"What do you mean, for how long?" he asked, looking blank.

"How long would you want me to live here with you?" she asked patiently, enunciating each word clearly.

"Ah." He squeezed her hand tighter. "Only as long as you want to stay, lady. As long as you want to stay."

She felt a sudden burst of hope. Her throat felt too choked up for her to speak.

"You can take your time, think about it," he said in a rush. "I know I can't ask you to marry me, though Lord knows I want to. I know you're too young to marry someone my age. But if you'd come here and live with me as long as you wanted, I'd let you go when you needed to have more freedom. I'd understand if you only wanted to stay a few months. Whatever time we can have together is all right with me." He paused and took a deep breath. "You said no before. It's damned audacious for me to ask you again, I know. But I had to try. Because I want you more than I've ever wanted anything in my whole life."

Her eyes brimmed with tears of joy, and her insides felt all light and bubbly. "I love you, Cole," she said.

His grip on her hand tightened convulsively, and he looked at her as if he hadn't heard her right.

"But I won't come live with you."

He dropped her hand, and the light died out of his eyes.

"I won't come live with you unless it's permanent. Unless we get married."

He lifted his eyes quickly to hers. "What are you saying?"

She rolled her eyes. "I can see you're going to make a dense husband," she said, grinning.

"Husband? You mean you'll—"

"I mean," she said with elaborate care, "that I'll marry you and live with you forever. And this 'too old' stuff is nonsense."

He was on his knees in front of her, pulling her to him and embracing her so tightly that she could hardly breathe. "Do you mean it? Do you mean it?"

"Of course I do," she said softly. "But Cole..."

"What, darling?"

"You're suffocating me."

He let her go, but kept a grip on her hands, looking hard at her face. "I was so sure you'd say no," he said. "I thought that you hated the thought of being with me. You were so decisive when I asked you to live with me before—"

"That's because you asked me to have an affair with you for a few months. I was too in love with you to do that. I knew I'd never survive the heartbreak of leaving you after I'd tasted what it was like to live with you."

He was looking into her eyes as if he couldn't believe what he'd heard her say. Clasping her to him again, he wrapped his arms around her tenderly, and they stayed in the embrace for long moments.

"You don't even know all the ways I thought of to sweeten the deal," he said finally.

"I don't know if it could be any sweeter."

"Well, let's see," he said, letting go of her to count on his fingers. "One, this place is only a couple of hours away from Crooked Fork, so you could go back there anytime you wanted to visit. Two, there's at least one college with a nursing program in Colorado Springs. So if you wanted to finish up your education, you could." He pulled her to her feet. "And number three you have to see. I can't describe it."

Mystified, she followed him as he led her toward the part of the house they hadn't yet explored. He threw open a door and gestured for her to go in first.

A skylight let the sun in, and one wall was made of glass. Outside, the mountain fell away in a sharp curve, leaving a clear view of a snowcapped range in the distance. An easel stood in the center of the room, and shelves and cupboards lined another wall. Atop the shelves were two framed drawings, and when she studied them, she saw that they were sketches she had done.

"Where did you get these?" she asked.

"At the souvenir shop in Crooked Fork," he said. "Well, do you like it? Do you think you could draw and paint here?"

He had fixed up this room for her! For her drawing. She whirled around, looking at everything, her heart pounding with excitement. "Cole, it'll be perfect!" she said. "It's the best studio anyone ever had!"

He drew her into his arms then, clasping her close against his broad chest. "So my enticements work, honey?"

She rested her face against his strength, closing her eyes. She could feel his heartbeat, strong and steady, and she was only beginning to realize that she was going to have the incredible joy of hearing that heartbeat, of feeling those strong arms around her, for the rest of her life.

"You didn't need to offer me any enticements," she murmured. "You were enough."

"Oh, Skye," he said hoarsely, running his hands through her hair. "I was so afraid you'd back away from me. I had to do anything I could to draw you closer. I've been setting this up for weeks, but after the other day I didn't think I'd ever get to show it to you."

Suddenly she remembered something. "But what about you, Cole?" she asked, pulling back so that she could look into his eyes. "What will you do? You're a city person. And what about Denton Rec?"

"It's going to work out fine," he said, smiling down at her. "We have another resort planned for just a couple of miles outside of Colorado Springs. With that and Crooked Fork, this part of the state is the real center of our business now. So we're moving from Denver to Colorado Springs. My brother and I made that decision a month ago, when we met in Denver."

"I can't believe things are working out so perfectly. I thought today would be the last day I'd see you."

Cole drew her to his side then, and they strolled slowly through the rest of the house. Cole pointed out some of its features, but mostly he concentrated his attention on her, stopping to kiss her and hold her every few steps. Skye felt her heart start to pound harder as his caresses grew more intense. His skilled hands wreaked havoc with her senses, until she was breathing hard in his arms. But now she didn't have to pull back, because when she looked up at him, the love shone from his eyes.

Finally he opened the last door. When she walked in, she couldn't help blushing. There was a huge, fully made bed, two night tables, bureaus, and an easy chair. And the carpet was so lush that her feet sank into it.

"So you decided to furnish this part of the house first, did you?" she asked him, teasing.

"I have my priorities in line," he said, putting his arms around her again. "I love you, lady," he whispered against her hair. "Lord, how I love you."

And as she let herself go in his arms, she knew that she'd found, in his love, the best home of all.

* * * * *

COMING NEXT MONTH

#682 RUN, ISABELLA—Suzanne Carey
Isabel Sloan had granted her father's last wish and married his handsome protégé, Max Darien. But did her new husband want her—or her father's legacy?

#683 THE PERFECT WIFE—Marcine Smith
Nona Alexander's first marriage had convinced her she wasn't meant for wedded bliss. But Nicholas Kendrick's ardent pursuit was quickly changing her mind!

#684 SWEET PROTECTOR—Patricia Ellis
Melanie Rogers saved Mac Chandler from kidnappers, nursed him to health and helped him solve a mystery. But once all the excitement settled down, would he follow suit?

#685 THIEF OF HEARTS—Beverly Terry
Tara Linton had unwittingly crossed paths with bumbling jewel thieves. Investigator Sam Miller made it his duty to protect her—and got his heart stolen right from under his nose!

#686 MOTHER FOR HIRE—Marie Ferrarella
Widower Bryan Marlowe knew that only a woman's touch could calm down his four mischievous sons, but new nanny Kate Llewellyn was wreaking havoc—on his heart....

#687 FINALLY HOME—Arlene James
Nicky Collier was chasing corporate secrets, and instead uncovered a love sweeter than she'd ever dreamed possible. Could she convince Gage Bardeen that she'd found what she'd really been looking for?

AVAILABLE THIS MONTH:

#676 A LOVE REMEMBERED
Annette Broadrick

#677 CONFIDENTIALLY YOURS
Helen R. Myers

#678 MOUNTAIN HOME
Erika Favor

#679 A KISS AND A PROMISE
Moyra Tarling

#680 RED SKY AT NIGHT
Octavia Street

#681 A GIFT FOR TENDERNESS
Peggy Webb

ANOTHER BRIDE FOR A BRANIGAN BROTHER!

Branigan's Touch
by Leslie Davis Guccione

Available in October 1989

You've written in asking for more about the Branigan brothers, so we decided to give you Jody's story—from *his* perspective.

Look for Mr. October—*Branigan's Touch*—a *Man of the Month*, coming from Silhouette Desire.

Following #311 *Bittersweet Harvest*, #353 *Still Waters* and #376 *Something in Common*, *Branigan's Touch* still stands on its own. You'll enjoy the warmth and charm of the Branigan clan—and watch the sparks fly when another Branigan man meets his match with an O'Connor woman!

SD523-1

INDULGE A LITTLE SWEEPSTAKES

OFFICIAL RULES

SWEEPSTAKES RULES AND REGULATIONS. NO PURCHASE NECESSARY.

1. NO PURCHASE NECESSARY. To enter complete the official entry form and return with the invoice in the envelope provided. Or you may enter by printing your name, complete address and your daytime phone number on a 3 x 5 piece of paper. Include with your entry the hand printed words "Indulge A Little Sweepstakes." Mail your entry to: Indulge A Little Sweepstakes, P.O. Box 1397, Buffalo, NY 14269-1397. No mechanically reproduced entries accepted. Not responsible for late, lost, misdirected mail, or printing errors.

2. Three winners, one per month (Sept. 30, 1989, October 31, 1989 and November 30, 1989), will be selected in random drawings. All entries received prior to the drawing date will be eligible for that month's prize. This sweepstakes is under the supervision of MARDEN-KANE, INC. an independent judging organization whose decisions are final and binding. Winners will be notified by telephone and may be required to execute an affidavit of eligibility and release which must be returned within 14 days, or an alternate winner will be selected.

3. Prizes: 1st Grand Prize (1) a trip for two to Disneyworld in Orlando, Florida. Trip includes round trip air transportation, hotel accommodations for seven days and six nights, plus up to $700 expense money (ARV $3,500). 2nd Grand Prize (1) a seven-night Chandris Caribbean Cruise for two includes transportation from nearest major airport, accommodations, meals plus up to $1,000 in expense money (ARV $4,300). 3rd Grand Prize (1) a ten-day Hawaiian holiday for two includes round trip air transportation for two, hotel accommodations, sightseeing, plus up to $1,200 in spending money (ARV $7,700). All trips subject to availability and must be taken as outlined on the entry form.

4. Sweepstakes open to residents of the U.S. and Canada 18 years or older except employees and the families of Torstar Corp., its affiliates, subsidiaries and Marden-Kane, Inc. and all other agencies and persons connected with conducting this sweepstakes. All Federal, State and local laws and regulations apply. Void wherever prohibited or restricted by law. Taxes, if any are the sole responsibility of the prize winners. Canadian winners will be required to answer a skill testing question. Winners consent to the use of their name, photograph and/or likeness for publicity purposes without additional compensation.

5. For a list of prize winners, send a stamped, self-addressed envelope to Indulge A Little Sweepstakes Winners, P.O. Box 701, Sayreville, NJ 08871.

DL-SWPS

INDULGE A LITTLE SWEEPSTAKES

OFFICIAL RULES

SWEEPSTAKES RULES AND REGULATIONS. NO PURCHASE NECESSARY.

1. NO PURCHASE NECESSARY. To enter complete the official entry form and return with the invoice in the envelope provided. Or you may enter by printing your name, complete address and your daytime phone number on a 3 x 5 piece of paper. Include with your entry the hand printed words "Indulge A Little Sweepstakes." Mail your entry to: Indulge A Little Sweepstakes, P.O. Box 1397, Buffalo, NY 14269-1397. No mechanically reproduced entries accepted. Not responsible for late, lost, misdirected mail, or printing errors.

2. Three winners, one per month (Sept. 30, 1989, October 31, 1989 and November 30, 1989), will be selected in random drawings. All entries received prior to the drawing date will be eligible for that month's prize. This sweepstakes is under the supervision of MARDEN-KANE, INC. an independent judging organization whose decisions are final and binding. Winners will be notified by telephone and may be required to execute an affidavit of eligibility and release which must be returned within 14 days, or an alternate winner will be selected.

3. Prizes: 1st Grand Prize (1) a trip for two to Disneyworld in Orlando, Florida. Trip includes round trip air transportation, hotel accommodations for seven days and six nights, plus up to $700 expense money (ARV $3,500). 2nd Grand Prize (1) a seven-night Chandris Caribbean Cruise for two includes transportation from nearest major airport, accommodations, meals plus up to $1,000 in expense money (ARV $4,300). 3rd Grand Prize (1) a ten-day Hawaiian holiday for two includes round trip air transportation for two, hotel accommodations, sightseeing, plus up to $1,200 in spending money (ARV $7,700). All trips subject to availability and must be taken as outlined on the entry form.

4. Sweepstakes open to residents of the U.S. and Canada 18 years or older except employees and the families of Torstar Corp., its affiliates, subsidiaries and Marden-Kane, Inc. and all other agencies and persons connected with conducting this sweepstakes. All Federal, State and local laws and regulations apply. Void wherever prohibited or restricted by law. Taxes, if any are the sole responsibility of the prize winners. Canadian winners will be required to answer a skill testing question. Winners consent to the use of their name, photograph and/or likeness for publicity purposes without additional compensation.

5. For a list of prize winners, send a stamped, self-addressed envelope to Indulge A Little Sweepstakes Winners, P.O. Box 701, Sayreville, NJ 08871.

© 1989 HARLEQUIN ENTERPRISES LTD.

DL-SWPS

INDULGE A LITTLE—WIN A LOT!

Summer of '89 Subscribers-Only Sweepstakes

OFFICIAL ENTRY FORM

This entry must be received by: Sept. 30, 1989
This month's winner will be notified by: October 7, 1989
Trip must be taken between: Nov. 7, 1989–Nov. 7, 1990

YES, I want to win the Walt Disney World® vacation for two! I understand the prize includes round-trip airfare, first-class hotel, and a daily allowance as revealed on the "Wallet" scratch-off card.

Name____________________

Address____________________

City__________ State/Prov._______ Zip/Postal Code_______

Daytime phone number____________________
Area code

Return entries with invoice in envelope provided. Each book in this shipment has two entry coupons—and the more coupons you enter, the better your chances of winning!

© 1989 HARLEQUIN ENTERPRISES LTD.

DINDL-1